QUEENS OF CYBERSPACE

REUNION TOUR

Clancy Teitelbaum

E

EPIC
Press

Reunion Tour
Queens of Cyberspace: Book #5

Written by Clancy Teitelbaum

Copyright © 2016 by Abdo Consulting Group, Inc.

Published by EPIC Press™
PO Box 398166
Minneapolis, MN 55439

Cover design by Laura Mitchell
Images for cover art obtained from iStockPhoto.com
Edited by Jennifer Skogen

LIBRARY OF CONGRESS CATALOGING-IN-PUBLICATION DATA

Teitelbaum, Clancy.
Reunion tour / Clancy Teitelbaum.
p. cm. — (Queens of cyberspace; #5)
Summary: For the first time since entering Io, the girls have been separated. The
girls will have to fight old enemies and former friends as they try to find a way back
together and back to reality.
ISBN 978-1-68076-201-3 (hardcover)
1. Friendship—Fiction. 2. Computer games—Fiction. 3. Internet—Fiction. 4.
Virtual reality—Fiction. 5. Cyberspace—Fiction. 6. Video games—Fiction. 7.
Young adult fiction. I. Title.
[Fic]—dc23
2015949427

EPICPRESS.COM

For the Borscht Belt Baron

Chapter 1

Suzanne noticed the chains as soon as she regained consciousness. Her wrists were shackled together. The chain connecting them ran through an iron rung bolted into the floor. She tried to lift her arms but couldn't raise them higher than her shoulder. She pulled on the chain, testing the strength of the rung. It didn't budge. She let her arms go limp.

Looking around her cell, she took in her new surroundings. There wasn't much to see. The walls, floor, and ceiling were all cut from the same drab stone. There was a mat on the floor, presumably where she was meant to sleep. No windows and a door made of iron bars. The only light came fit-fully from a torch in a wall sconce. Suzanne took a few steps toward the door before the chain started to pull her arms through her legs. She stopped, took a step back, and sat down as gracefully as her bonds would allow.

This cell wasn't her first. While awaiting trial with Brit and Mikayla, Suzanne was treated to the finest dungeon in Zenith City. But she couldn't be in Zenith City now. No, the stone that formed her cell was the same stone that made up all the towers and halls of Fenhold, the southern stronghold of King Ramses.

In Zenith City, Suzanne had picked the locks on their bonds to escape. That was one of her special talents as she played the game as an Infiltrator. So she turned her wrists over, searching her shackles for a keyhole. As soon as she found one she would be able to initiate a lock-picking mini-game, which was basically a sliding block puzzle.

But search as she might, she couldn't find the

keyhole. Whoever put them on her must have forged them shut around her wrists. Which was impossible as far as Suzanne knew. And she knew a lot about this world, Io, considering she had designed the entire game.

In reality, Suzanne was in her bedroom, wearing a Total Immersion Interface. Brit and Mikayla were also in her room. To anyone watching they'd appear to be asleep, immersed in some active dream. Time moved at different speeds in Io, so Suzanne had no idea how many real-world hours it had been since the girls were stuck in the virtual world.

And they were stuck in Io, like Suzanne was stuck in this cell. She ran her fingers over every inch of her shackles, in case she missed something. The metal was cool and rough and seamless. This was getting her nowhere. She would have thrown her hands up in disgust if she was able.

Suzanne heard footsteps coming toward her. She scrambled back up on her feet. If it was Ramses, coming to gloat over having captured her, Suzanne wanted to face the NPC standing. Ramses was the one who lured Suzanne and her friends to the swampy Fens that covered the southern part of Altair. But even before that, the king was the NPC responsible for all of the girls' misery since becoming trapped in Io.

Suzanne leaned back against the cell wall, crossing her arms as best as she could in an effort to look nonchalant. It wasn't Ramses. Instead, a Monk strolled in front of Suzanne's cell. Her plain leather armor was branded with the sigil of Altairi—four pillars and a crimson orb. The sigil stood for Zenith City, Ramses's former capital. Fenhold was where he had come after Suzanne, Brit, and Mikayla drove him from his throne.

The Monk stopped in front of Suzanne's cell. She was, Suzanne noticed, staying more than an arm's length away. The Monk hardly looked at Suzanne. She peered at the edges of the cell, looking, Suzanne guessed, for something out of place.

"Let me out of here," Suzanne said. She tried to sound calm but firm, like Mikayla would.

The only response she got was a wide smile.

Well, it was worth a shot. Changing her approach, Suzanne asked, "Where are my friends? Where's Brit and Mikayla?"

Still the only response she got was the smile.

"Look," Suzanne said, "I get that Ramses is your king and everything. But you can at least tell me where I am, right? What's going to happen to me?"

The Monk, evidently satisfied, disappeared back down the hallway.

Three more NPCs came that day. By the time the last one arrived, Suzanne wasn't even bothering to stand anymore. She was already locked in a cell so it wasn't like she could intimidate anyone.

First came a Sellsword, his weapon out as if Suzanne might break free at any moment. His hands were shaking so much it looked like he might drop his sword. As soon as Suzanne opened her mouth he fled in terror.

The second NPC to come was someone she had seen before. He was a hulking Dragoon, a rattling mountain of plate mail and muscle. His name was Crux and he had been the captain of the Zenith City Guard and a champion of Altair in the war.

"Hello," Suzanne said.

"Hello," the giant replied in his deep voice.

He had a simple face, making him look like an overgrown child. And unlike the other NPCs, he wasn't looking around her cell, but looking right at her.

"Your name's Crux, right? Can you tell me where I am?"

He shook his head no. "I'm not supposed to talk to you," he said. Then he frowned, realizing that he just had spoken to her. He trundled off down the hallway.

Last was a Barbarian with a horned helmet and long beard. As he turned back down the hallway, Suzanne called after him.

"Who are you? Where am I?"

The Barbarian came back into view. "My name's Karter," he said in a gruff voice. "I'm the deputy jailer. And you're in the dungeons of Fenhold. Get as comfortable as you can. You'll be here until the king figures out what to do with you.

"And I almost forgot," he added. He extinguished the torch and stomped off down the hallway, leaving Suzanne alone in the dark.

She waited a few hours after Karter left, but no other NPCs came. If she was just going to sit in the dark, she might as well try to get some sleep. Without a window to the outside world, she couldn't tell if it was night or not, but she lay down on the sleeping mat anyway.

When she closed her eyes she saw a sickly green light. Her eyes flew open and she spasmed back to sitting. The green light reminded her of the chamber beneath Fenhold where she found King Ramses and Xenos. She felt nauseous all of a sudden. But that was impossible, seeing as Suzanne hadn't programmed nausea into Io. Just like her shackles were impossible.

Suzanne sighed. When Xenos was involved, things tended to stop making sense. Suzanne could still picture him in that weird chamber, his hood pulled low over his face as always. Xenos had reached out toward Ramses with a glowing hand and the King had parroted everything Xenos said, like he was hypnotized. Then Gemini, Ramses's pet Assassin, had come out of nowhere attacking Suzanne. When Suzanne tried to fight back, Xenos had shut her down, and then she had passed out.

That was the last thing she remembered before waking up in her cell. She rustled her chains, but they still didn't yield. She'd have to wait for Brit and Mikayla to come rescue her.

When she woke up, the torch was relit. Someone must have come by while she was sleeping. Well, if they hadn't killed her while she was asleep, she was probably safe for the immediate future. Safe and secure, locked in her cell.

First, the Monk. As before, she was all smiles

and no words. Then the shaking Sellsword, then Crux the Dragoon, and finally Karter the Barbarian. This time when she tried to talk to Karter he ignored her, extinguishing the torch and leaving as quickly as he could.

Suzanne wasn't tired at all, so she waited up to see who had relit the torch. But at some point in the night the torch simply relit itself. Suzanne jumped in surprise, but as far as Io went, self-lighting torches were pretty tame.

By now Suzanne was becoming suspicious that Brit and Mikayla weren't coming. They must have gone looking for her when they discovered she was missing. She imagined them scouring the castle, kicking in doors and shaking down NPCs until they found her. The thought of Brit throwing Ramses around was particularly satisfying.

But at the start of her third day in captivity, Suzanne had to admit to her doubts. She wondered if Ramses had captured her friends, too. She remembered Xenos telling Ramses to "Get rid of the other two," and Suzanne didn't want to think about what that meant. To get to Ramses, Brit and Mikayla would have to go through an entire castle full of soldiers, and Xenos. Just thinking about him made Suzanne shudder. It would be better if Brit and Mikayla didn't fight the hooded NPC at all.

Maybe they realized they couldn't win the fight and went to find help. Rigel had been at the summit; maybe Brit and Mikayla had gone with him back to Pyxis. Suzanne had fought for Pyxis in the war against Altair. She figured that the Pyxians wouldn't let her rot in one of Ramses's dungeons. Especially not Leo, the Pyxian king.

Suzanne hardly noticed the Monk and the Sellsword's visits, but at some point in the afternoon she realized that the Dragoon Crux had not yet stopped by her cell. He normally came well before the Barbarian. So far he was a no-show.

She heard two sets of footsteps and then a conversation. "If you don't mind me asking, sir, what do you come up here for?"

That sounded like Karter. Sure enough, the Barbarian came into view, followed by Crux.

"Me and Porter and Helga can keep an eye on her," Karter said. "It's not like she's going anywhere."

Crux thought for a minute before answering. "It sets me at ease checking on her myself, Karter. This one has given Altair no shortage of trouble."

"Fair enough," Karter said. "Make sure you put out the torch when you go." With a cursory glance over the cell, the Barbarian left.

Crux watched him go. Once it was clear that he had gone, the Dragoon turned back toward Suzanne. His eyes searched her face and tried to coolly return their gaze.

"Do you know who Burgrave is?" he asked her.

Of course she knew who Burgrave was. He was a short NPC, a fierce fighter, and absolutely loyal to Ramses. Burgrave had been the first member of Ramses's court that she and her friends had met. Crux had been there that day, in his role as the captain of the guard.

Suzanne didn't answer his question. Even if he wasn't one of her jailers, he was still Ramses's stooge, and she didn't owe him anything.

Crux frowned. "You do not wish to speak with me. This I understand. We are enemies, you and I. It is natural for us not to help each other."

Suzanne wondered what he was getting at.

"No one will tell me where Burgrave is," Crux said sadly. At that moment he looked like an overgrown child, searching for a parent. Despite herself, Suzanne felt sorry for the giant Dragoon.

She dimly remembered seeing Burgrave leave Fenhold the night she was captured. Suzanne had assumed that Burgrave was off on some mission for Ramses. Why did Crux think she would know where Burgrave had gone?

He stared at her a moment longer. Suzanne realized she could plug the NPC for information. She never liked those parts of games where you had to navigate lengthy conversations, choosing the right line of dialogue to get NPCs to spill the beans.

When designing Io, she had done her best to leave dialogue trees out of the game. But there wasn't much else she could do right now, and besides, she was feeling a little starved for attention.

"I saw Burgrave right before they captured me," she said.

The Dragoon's face lit up with excitement. "Where?" he asked, nearly shouting.

"Keep it down," Suzanne cautioned. "I don't think we're supposed to be talking."

Crux looked so chastened she almost laughed. "Where did you see him?" he whispered.

"He was leaving the castle. I watched him go out into the swamp, but I didn't follow him."

Crux pondered her words before asking, "Was he alone?"

"As far as I could tell."

The Dragoon frowned and sat himself heavily upon the floor of the hallway. Even sitting, his body filled most of the door frame. The Dragoon put his head in his hands, muffling his voice as he asked, "Why did he go? Why didn't he take me with him?"

Suzanne didn't know what to say. "Maybe he had to take care of something important?" she suggested. "He looked like he was in a hurry."

Crux shook his head. "Ramses stopped sending him on missions. He said Burgrave was helping more by watching over things here. I heard them arguing about it, but Burgrave told me not to worry."

He looked straight at Suzanne. "Should I have worried? Did the fighting make Burgrave want to run away?"

That didn't sound like Burgrave to Suzanne; he was obedient to a fault. But if he had been fighting with Ramses it could be a sign that Burgrave had had enough of the king's bullshit. Would he just run away, though?

Suzanne's gut told her no. Once, Burgrave explained to Suzanne his philosophy on life. The NPC claimed that he served Ramses in order to help as many Altairi as possible. He had already put up with some pretty loathsome shit, so why would he suddenly make a break for it now?

Unless it hadn't been Ramses who drove Burgrave away.

"Crux," she said gently. The Dragoon looked up at her. "Did Burgrave tell you anything about Xenos?"

Crux flinched at the name. "Burgrave didn't like him," he said.

Well, duh, Suzanne thought. "Why not?"

"He said . . ." Crux began, and then cut himself off, as if he had thought the better of it. "I have to go," he whispered. "We can talk more tomorrow. Will you meet me here?"

He was gone before Suzanne could point out the absurdity of his question. Despite the shackles around her wrists and ankles, despite how ridiculous her situation had become, Suzanne began to laugh. Of course she would meet him here tomorrow. It wasn't like she had another choice.

Chapter 2

"We should go back," Mikayla said.

They were in a small glen off the side of the road. The trees were thick enough that Mikayla and Brit were hidden from anyone traveling on the road. Mikayla insisted that they hide themselves while resting.

Brit opened her eyes and stared at Mikayla. Mikayla's character looked way more like her real world body than Brit's or Suzanne's. She was an athlete in the real world, and as a Swiftblade, Mikayla possessed the same lean, muscular frame. Brit's avatar, on the other hand, was about two feet taller and several dozen pounds of muscle bigger than Brit in the real world.

Mikayla was dressed in a traveling cloak with the hood pulled up over her head, which was something Mikayla would never wear in real life. She was sitting with her arms wrapped around her knees, curled up like she was trying to make herself as small as possible. She wasn't looking at Brit, but at her knees. Brit could hear her voice shaking. She wondered if Mikayla's whole body would shake if she didn't hold herself so tightly.

"We should go back," Mikayla repeated. Brit looked away, hoping Mikayla would take the hint and drop it. Off in the distance she could see a band of kobolds scavenging for food. She longed to chase them down and bash their lizard heads in. She had plenty of anger to work off. But there was no time for that now; they were only resting to catch their breath and then they'd set off again. The kobolds evidently found something worth eating. Brit turned away as the band pounced on their sorry prey.

"We should go back," Mikayla said again, a little louder.

Brit sighed. This was the fifth time Mikayla had said they should go back. Today. It sucked being the reasonable one.

"We can't go back," Brit said. "You know we can't go back. You told me we couldn't go back when we were still in the Fenlands, remember?"

Brit remembered well enough.

The two of them had smashed through the window of Ramses's castle to escape, barely making it out of the courtyard alive. Brit's armor was full of arrows. Some had broken through. She could feel them in her arms and legs as they ran.

They kept running until Fenhold was lost behind the swamp's dense foliage. Brit stopped. She had lost too much health and her health bar would keep dropping if they didn't take the arrows out. Brit didn't flinch as Mikayla ripped them free. She pulled out the last one herself.

Snapping the shaft in two, Brit said, "We have to go back."

"We can't," Mikayla replied, pleading. She looked as miserable as Brit felt.

But Brit was in no mood to split and run. "We can't just leave Suzanne there!" she shouted.

"What are you going to do? Ramses has an army, Brit. If we get captured then who's going to come rescue us?"

Brit knew Mikayla was right but that didn't help the anger building inside her. She let out a wordless yell of rage and slammed her fist into a tree. The bark splintered beneath her punch and the tree fell over, sending a flock of swamp gulls flapping away in fear.

"We can't just leave Suzanne," Brit repeated, her voice barely more than a whisper.

But they had left her. That was two days ago. Two days of hard traveling, day and night. They chased the sunsets west toward Pyxis. After the first day they were clear of the Fens, picking up speed as the ground hardened and sloped downwards toward the shore of the Ion River.

They took turns with the watch at night. Asleep, Mikayla's face was perfectly calm, the resting face of any character in game. Brit wished Mikayla could feel that calm while she was awake. She wondered if Mikayla, like her, could dream in the game. Suzanne had told them that they wouldn't dream in Io, and yet, Brit dreamt vividly and often. She hadn't told Suzanne about these dreams because she didn't want to answer a million different questions about them. She couldn't always remember her dreams, but what she did remember was definitely not stuff she wanted to discuss with Suzanne. And she didn't tell Mikayla either.

Now that it was just the two of them, it felt like the perfect time to talk about her dreams. But Brit hadn't, deciding they had enough on their minds already. They only stopped when exhaustion compelled them to collapse. They were racing against a clock they couldn't read to hit a deadline they couldn't miss.

And now Mikayla was balking, saying they should go back. She had been quiet ever since they left the Fens, but today she seemed particularly on edge. Still, Brit never expected Mikayla to flip-flop like this.

Brit told Mikayla what Mikayla had told her when they were still in the Fens.

"You told me we had to get backup. We're getting backup. We're going to catch up with Rigel and bring half of fucking Pyxis back with us. We're going to knock Fenhold down and beat the shit out of Ramses and rescue Suzanne and live happily ever fucking after, okay?"

Mikayla kept staring at her knees and muttered something Brit couldn't hear.

"What was that?"

"I was wrong. We shouldn't have left her."

Brit laughed out loud in amazement. "You, wrong?"

Brit knew it was a mistake as soon as she said it. The transformation in Mikayla was instantaneous. Her back stiffened and she finally looked away from her knees, shooting a glare at Brit.

"You don't need to be such a bitch," Mikayla snapped.

Brit wanted nothing more than to blow this up into an argument, but that would waste time they didn't have. Being the reasonable one really sucked.

"Fine," Brit said. "It's time to move on anyway."

It was a clear and brisk day, but to Brit it seemed like they were traveling under a storm cloud regardless. Mikayla only broke the silence to warn Brit of monsters or obstacles up ahead. But Brit noticed Mikayla was omitting certain things: Mikayla didn't warn her about a shallow ditch, and she didn't offer Brit a hand back up when Brit tripped over the ditch and fell.

And you think I'm being bitchy. But Brit didn't call her out. They didn't have time to waste arguing. If Mikayla wanted to stay and fight, why couldn't they have done that in the first place? The days of traveling had convinced Brit that splitting had been the right choice. It was shitty to do that to Suzanne, but Brit knew she could handle herself. Back in the real world, Brit had watched queen bitch Gretchen and her bitchlings dump on Suzanne for a year. If Suze could take their bullshit, then she could last a few more days in Ramses's dungeon.

It's only going to be a few more days, Brit told herself. If they kept up this pace they would be in New Pyxia the day after tomorrow. And Leo had to help them. The last time Brit had seen the prince—no, he was a king now—he still had a huge hard-on for Suzanne. Even if distance and time had cooled him off a little, he had to help them out, right?

It all struck Brit as perversely funny—Mikayla being so unreasonable while she was the one pushing them away from a fight. And their grand plan to rescue Suzanne hinged entirely on an NPC's inability to get over an ex.

What a weird fucking game, Brit thought.

On Mikayla's insistence, they steered clear of every town. Mikayla could see way better than Brit, so Brit took her word for it whenever Mikayla said it was time to get off the road.

Brit didn't think it was necessary to be so cautious. They'd only be in trouble if they ran into an NPC who both served Ramses and recognized the two of them. Even then, Brit wasn't really afraid of NPCs. It wasn't like they would run into an army wandering the Altairi countryside.

Every time they left the road they lost a ton of time, but Mikayla insisted. On reflection, Brit realized Mikayla had been insisting a lot of things lately. Maybe she was still shaken up by how things had gone down at Fenhold. Everything had gone well enough at first, or at least as well as things could go with Ramses involved. But after Suzanne disappeared the whole summit had blown up in their faces.

First, the Pyxian delegation left, and then Ramses had framed them for killing all of Lady Mara's subjects, when in fact the Assassin Gemini had led the massacre. Brit had liked Mara. She was about as good as NPCs got, but when the shit hit the fan Mikayla ended up dueling the Paladin, and Mara lost.

Brit knew Mikayla. She'd known Mikayla since they were little, and going that far back Mikayla had never been big into hurting others. She wouldn't even step on bugs, instead squealing for Brit to get rid of them. Brit always pretended to take them outside but really she'd just squish the bugs in a tissue and get on with her day.

Even if Brit thought Mikayla was a bit of a wimp back then, Mikayla was still her best friend. Before they knew Suzanne, Mikayla provided Brit's one refuge from domineering parents.

Mikayla's behavior wasn't just annoying Brit. It hurt her to see her friend acting like this. Acting like someone else entirely. Brit might have literally changed the way she looked while playing in Io, but she didn't want the game to change how Mikayla acted.

The sun was beginning to set when Mikayla stopped walking.

"We can't go back," Brit said.

"I wasn't going to say that," Mikayla coldly replied. "But we should stop here for the night. We've got good vantage on the surrounding area so we'll be able to see anyone coming."

Brit laughed. "See who coming? It's going to be dark out, and I can't see in the dark like you can. Are you going to take the watch all night?"

"Maybe I should," Mikayla said. "If that's what it takes to keep us safe."

"You're nuts," Brit said. But she took her tent out of her inventory and set it up. She was feeling tired herself, and they could always get an early start tomorrow.

Brit could feel Mikayla watching her. Eventually Mikayla began to set up her own tent. When they were both done, they sat in silence until it was dark. Once the sun was completely gone, Brit said, "You take first watch, and I'll take second."

"Brit . . . " Mikayla's voice trailed off.

"What?"

Mikayla hesitated, like she was about to say something else. Brit waited, but Mikayla couldn't seem to put the words together.

Brit turned toward her tent. "Call me if anyone shows up," she said. "Wake me up when it's my turn to take watch." She ducked inside the tent and let the flap fall shut behind her. Maybe Mikayla would know what to say in the morning.

Chapter 3

Suzanne waited. She hated how helpless she was. She had designed this entire world, and she was stuck in a jail cell with nothing else to do but wait for Crux. Yesterday, despite her best efforts to steer the conversation elsewhere, they ended up talking about his favorite subject—Burgrave.

"Do you think Burgrave will come back soon?" was Crux's repeated question.

Suzanne wanted to tell him she had no idea. Instead, she gave specious answers. "He'll be back once he's finished his mission," she told him. "He's probably helping out Citizens," was another reply. Once, she even suggested that Burgrave was staying away so long to give Crux a chance to grow into his own. But that leap in logic proved to be too much for the Dragoon, but Suzanne didn't know what else she could tell him.

The truth was Suzanne was becoming a little curious about Burgrave's whereabouts herself. She overheard two of her other jailers discussing the missing advisor.

"King said we weren't going looking for him," Porter the Sellsword said. "King said Burgrave was working some special deal, very secret."

Karter the Barbarian barked a curt laugh. "'Course he would say that. Ramses can't very well admit Burgrave's gone and split, now can he?"

"Like you know that."

"I do," Karter insisted. "Heard him speaking with Xenos about it. 'He's dead to us,' that Xenos said."

"Then what?"

"Then I made myself scarce! You telling me you would've stuck around and let the King and Xenos find you there? Now hush up before the prisoner hears us."

"You don't need to tell me to hush up," Porter grumbled, but by the time they arrived in front of her cell both Sellsword and Barbarian were as tight-lipped as ever. Suzanne had noticed that Porter was less afraid of her when he had the Barbarian around for back up. Since Crux was checking up on her in the evenings, the two of them had begun to visit her cell together.

Karter gave Suzanne's cell a quick once-over. Satisfied, they left, resuming their conversation just out of earshot. She could hear Karter laughing about something as they descended the tower stairs.

But soon enough Crux came by, ready as usual to talk about Burgrave. And he did talk, so much so that Suzanne hardly got a word in. She never imagined Crux was capable of so much conversation. Before her imprisonment, the Dragoon had struck her as all muscle, another obedient soldier of Altair. It wasn't like Crux had shown her a revolutionary side, but he had made it abundantly clear that his desire to serve the king stemmed directly from a desire to help Burgrave.

"Burgrave is from Pyxis," Suzanne said, when the Dragoon paused to catch his breath. "How come you trust him so much?"

"Burgrave's parents are from Pyxis," Crux corrected her. "He told me that they were from a town called Glensia. Burgrave said he wanted to go back there one day, but that was before the war."

Suzanne wondered if Burgrave was in Glensia now. That was as good of a guess as anywhere else in Io. But they had talked about Burgrave long enough.

"Listen," Suzanne said, "I need your help. We'll make a trade, okay? You let me out of here and I'll help you find Burgrave."

"I cannot," Crux said. He crossed his arms and turned his back to her.

Suzanne thought he looked like an overgrown baby. But she couldn't give up on him, couldn't shout at him for being an idiot, no matter how much she wanted to. She needed Crux. He was the only NPC in Fenhold she could trust—if she could, indeed, trust him.

"Come on," she began, but Crux cut her off.

"King Ramses says you are to remain locked up," he sniffed. "I will not disobey a direct order from King Ramses."

He turned around to glare at her and then resumed his cross-armed huffiness.

"Listen," she said, afraid he might clap his hands over his ears and start singing to block her out. "You don't know where Burgrave went. Let me help you find him."

Crux started to turn back but caught himself. "You said you did not know where he was."

I don't, Suzanne thought. She had a couple of guesses, though, and all of those guesses led to Pyxis. She just wouldn't be as honest with Crux as she was with herself. He would only find out she had misled him when she ditched him in the wilderness.

"That's because if I told you," Suzanne said, "then you'd just go find him and then I'd still be here. That's not fair, is it?"

For a moment, Crux was silent. Then slowly, almost reluctantly, he turned to face her again. He was deep in thought, torn—it was written clearly on his face—between his desires for finding Burgrave and following orders.

"I could check on your information," Crux said slowly. "If it is correct then I will return and free you."

Suzanne gritted her teeth. *He's trying*, she reminded herself.

She tried to speak gently as she explained. "That won't work. What if something happens to you while you're gone, and I'm left here forever? I want to help you."

She could see he was falling for it. Or at least she hoped he was. She felt a little bad misleading Crux, but her sympathy for Ramses's soldiers only extended so far.

Then Suzanne heard footsteps growing louder. She

couldn't be sure, but it sounded like way more than the usual one or two NPCs. And indeed it was: a group of guards passed in front of her cell, long pikes streaming banners with the Altairi insignia. Suzanne had gone so long without seeing colors that to her, the crimson pillars and orb appeared to be glowing.

The NPCs turned and stood at attention. Crux turned and saluted the assembly. Suzanne thought they looked pretty stupid. *What do they think I'm going to do?* she wondered. *If I could break out of here, I would have done it by now.*

A lanky figure loped between the guards: King Ramses. His crown sat crooked on his head. More than anything, his pale face looked exhausted. The usual smirk was gone.

"Suzanne," he said, his voice cold with disdain.

Well, at least some things are normal, Suzanne thought. She didn't speak back to him; she didn't have anything to say. Suzanne would have never imagined she could loathe anything she had created as much as she loathed Ramses.

The king turned to Crux. "What are you doing here?"

Crux said nothing. His whole body was quivering with fear.

Ramses stared at him a moment longer before losing interest.

"I have come," Ramses drawled, unfazed by her silence, "to ask for information. If you help me I may be inclined to ease your confinement."

Suzanne couldn't help the laugh that escaped from her. "You might be inclined? Are you fucking kidding me? How about you let me out of this cell and I'll answer any question you have, right after I'm done knocking the shit out of you."

"An answer I might expect from your friend, Brit. Be reasonable, girl. The most you can hope for is my kindness. You would do well not to test the limits of my humor."

If Suzanne had any inclination to see what Ramses wanted it went out the window when he spat the word *girl* at her. She wasn't going to stand condescension from a video game character.

"You are only still alive because of my mercy," Ramses said.

"Really?" Suzanne replied. "Here I was, thinking you were just following Xenos's orders."

To her satisfaction, an angry red blotch blossomed on Ramses's face.

"He does not command me!" Ramses shouted. "I am the king!"

But for Suzanne that just confirmed her suspicions. In the underground chamber it had looked like Xenos was controlling Ramses, and the king's outburst told Suzanne that Ramses had some idea of what was going on. That only gave her more questions about Xenos, but she knew one thing for certain now: Ramses was afraid of him too.

After a moment of discomposure, Ramses managed to wrangle his emotions. "Perhaps I have been uncouth."

"Perhaps?" But Suzanne held back from saying

more. It was fun to antagonize Ramses, but if he was willing to bear her insults then he must really need her help. She might as well hear what he had to say.

"You do not trust me. I understand this. We are enemies, Suzanne of elsewhere. But you must know that this world is larger than you are. Even if it has increased the enmity between us, all I have done, I have done for the good of Altair."

The earnestness in his voice surprised Suzanne. She would have never pegged Ramses for an altruist. Yet how could his war with Pyxis have been good for anyone? The war had destabilized his country entirely, and Ramses had abandoned most of it, leaving Zenith City to fend for itself.

"For a long time, I imagined I had one subject who viewed matters in much the same way as I did. Burgrave was essential to my reign, my right hand. Yet now he has disappeared. And so I ask you, where has Burgrave gone?"

Burgrave again? She glanced at Crux, but he was staring directly at the king. Suzanne looked

Ramses straight in the eye and told him the truth. "I don't know where Burgrave is," she said.

"Think carefully," Ramses said. "I need to find him. As I said, I will reward you for your help. Any information you have can only improve your situation."

"And as I said, I have no idea where he is. Maybe if you spent less time starting wars and more time watching your court, you would know where he went."

"I will ignore that," Ramses said, but by his cheeks flushing it didn't seem likely he would. "Burgrave possesses an item of utmost importance to me. As much as I value his council, it is this item I truly require."

"Wow. That really sucks," Suzanne said. She couldn't help herself.

"I trusted him completely and he betrayed me."

"Do you remember when we first came to Zenith City?" Suzanne asked him. "We offered you our services and you accepted, saying you would reward us generously for our help. Instead, you framed us for murder and threw us in a dungeon. Don't you think people would trust you more if, you know, you ever kept your word? Like just once?"

"Is my word more important than my people?" Ramses demanded. "You think you are so wise, but you are just a child! There are forces at play in this land that you could never hope to understand. I have had to sacrifice so much for my people, and do they thank me for it? No! They exalt you and your ilk, and demonize me. Yet these same Citizens owe me everything! Everything!"

Suzanne could see some of the guards shifting uneasily as the king spat out his tirade. Realizing they were not alone, Ramses stood up, straightened his crown, and once more tried to master his emotions.

"Leave us," he said to the guards.

The guards hesitated. A Paladin stepped forward, asking in a timid voice, "Is it safe to leave you alone, my lord?"

"Fine. Crux stays, the rest of you go. Now go!"

The Paladin saluted and led the rest of the guards away. They moved quickly. Suzanne thought they were happy to get far away from the ranting king.

As soon as they were gone, Ramses dropped his shoulders and slumped into the wall. To Suzanne, he looked older, ancient.

"He has the key to the Oracle Chamber," Ramses said.

Her heart skipped a beat.

"I cannot access the room," Ramses said. "I cannot . . . " He glanced at her suspiciously. As far as Ramses knew, Suzanne had no idea what the room was, what it was capable of. Once upon a time he had promised to use it to send her and her friends home. But that was all he had told her.

"Of course you can't," Suzanne said. "It's in Zenith City."

Ramses smiled. "How little you know," he said.

How little you know, Suzanne thought. Ramses didn't know it, but the Oracle Chamber was a hack point Suzanne had designed. It was her backdoor out of the game, a fail-safe in case anything went wrong. If she got into the Oracle Chamber she could alter the game's code from within, giving her and her friends a way out. The only problem was that the Oracle Chamber had a lock. Suzanne hadn't put it there and she hadn't been able to open it either, despite a month of trying back in Zenith City. If Ramses was still trying to get into it, then either he had moved the Chamber using its own power or the key was some kind of warping item.

"We may have a common interest," Ramses continued. "If you retrieve this key for me, I will send you home."

"What do you need from there anyway?" Suzanne asked.

"There is something I need to deal with," Ramses said. "I need to access the Oracle Chamber. Once I do, that Xenos—" He cut himself off.

I knew it! Suzanne thought. Whoever Xenos was, Ramses couldn't control the hooded NPC much longer. Underlying her satisfaction, she couldn't help wondering what Xenos had done to make Ramses so afraid. Or maybe Ramses remembered what had happened in the tunnels beneath Fenhold, and he was trying to deal with the NPC before it was too late.

"I need to get into the Chamber," Ramses repeated. "And you will help me."

"And if I don't?" Suzanne asked.

"Then I see no purpose in continuing to host you here in my castle," the king replied. The old sneer feel back into place. Ramses, king of Altair, walked away. Crux followed after his liege, giving Suzanne one look before he went. The Dragoon looked shocked by Ramses's threat.

Suzanne felt electric. Her confinement had dulled her mind, but it was once again firing on all cylinders. Ramses might think that they shared a common interest, but Suzanne knew better. As soon as she got out of this cell, she'd go find Burgrave. Then she'd be able to escape Io once and for all.

Chapter 4

As they approached the river the next morning, Mikayla got a face full of acid. They were fighting a pack of skunkas, a rather territorial mix between giant sloths and skunks that sprayed a corrosive fluid instead of stink. Brit was grappling with a skunka while Mikayla finished another monster off.

The thing about skunkas was that they exploded when you finished knocking them out. And they didn't just explode into pixels like every other monster. No, dying skunkas also blasted out burning gunk equivalent to their current Energite reserve.

Which, in the case of the one Brit knocked off, happened to be a lot.

Brit threw herself out of the way without warning Mikayla. Mikayla was focused on dodging her skunka's swiping claws, her back to Brit. She heard the crackle that preceded the explosion and turned around in time to get smacked in the face by a glob.

She watched her health bar drop away. Skunka venom had to be cleansed immediately or it would continue to burn, so she retreated from the fight to search her inventory for a healing item. A few herbs and an elixir later and Mikayla's health bar was completely restored.

Her mood, however, was not. Mikayla tried to hold back her anger, but after half an hour of traveling she couldn't contain herself anymore.

"You should have warned me!" Mikayla said. She tried to keep her tone level, but Brit really had screwed her over.

"Whatever," Brit replied. "You're fine."

"Now I'm fine."

"And you were fine then! A few items and you're as good as new."

"That's not the point," Mikayla replied. "We have to look out for each other!

"Dude, drop it. You're freaking out over nothing!"

They were far enough north now that the Grand Highway was a real road again. The first time Mikayla saw the Highway it was filled with NPCs traveling north to Zenith City. She had been stunned by the spectacle of the crowd.

But ever since the Pyxian-Altairi War, the Highway was looking worse for the wear. Now there were potholes as big as ponds punched into the road and weeds choked the path in some places. It wasn't a big deal, as they'd only be on the Highway for a little longer, but having to hack through tall grass only soured her mood.

"I'm not freaking out over nothing," Mikayla said. Her anger slowed her speech, making her enunciate each syllable. "But we are trapped in a world where everything wants to kill us. We don't know what happens when we die. So when you tell me I'm freaking out over nothing, it makes me wonder what the fuck is wrong with you!"

She shouted the last few words. Hopefully, Brit would get the message.

And then Brit rolled her eyes. Mikayla seriously considered stabbing her.

"That's exactly what I'm talking about," Brit was saying. "You don't need to be so pressed on death all the time. Freaking out won't fix everything. So there are monsters. So Ramses wants to kill us. So we could die. Who gives a shit?"

"Who gives a shit?" Mikayla asked, full of disbelief. "Who gives a shit? I give a shit! Sorry that I'm worried about my life."

"Okay," Brit said, "I didn't mean—"

Mikayla didn't let her finish. "Sorry I'm trying to rescue Suzanne."

"Hey," Brit said, anger creeping into her voice, "that's completely un—"

"You never give a shit about anything!" Mikayla roared. She had never yelled at Brit like this before, but it felt long overdue. "You don't give a shit about what anyone does or says or thinks. You only give a shit about what you want!"

Mikayla could hear the Ion River off in the distance. She wasn't looking at Brit now, just staring at the road ahead. After about twenty steps, she realized Brit had stopped walking and turned back to see her standing dazed in the middle of the road.

"I give a shit what you think," Brit said. "How could you not think that?"

She stumbled back into a walk.

Mikayla's anger broke against the expression on Brit's face. Guilt surged into its place. Mikayla had never yelled at Brit like this and she had never made Brit feel like this. She didn't even think she could. Brit looked like she looked after a particularly nasty fight with her mom. She wasn't angry or sullen or resentful, but defeated. And Mikayla never wanted to make Brit feel that way.

But just because her anger deflated, Mikayla didn't think she was wrong. She couldn't keep yelling now, that part had burned out, yet she couldn't just turn on a dime and apologize for what she had said. As they neared the Ion River, Mikayla sought a way to explain herself.

"Do you remember when we played *Resident Evil 4*?" Mikayla asked.

"Yeah," Brit muttered.

"You know I hated that game, right?"

Brit stared at her in amazement. "But you bought it. We played through the entire thing together."

"No," Mikayla said, with a smile. "You played through the entire thing. I was too scared. I had to keep covering my eyes with my hands, especially when the cultists started exploding into tentacle monsters."

"I'm sorry," Brit said. "I never knew."

Mikayla shrugged. "You really liked that game.

And I figured I could take it. But that's what I'm talking about. You can't do that anymore."

Brit frowned. Mikayla knew she teetering on the edge of lecturing.

"And," Mikayla added, "I probably need to calm down a little."

She laughed. At first it sounded stilted, but then genuine chuckles broke out. After a moment, Brit laughed a little, too.

They laughed as the path led them through a shallow wood. Every step, the sound of rushing water grew louder, until they emerged from the wood onto the bank of the chuckling Ion River.

"I could've sworn you liked that game," Brit said.

"I liked some of the boss fights," Mikayla replied. "Even if they were a little gross."

Even if they were feeling better, they still didn't have a way across the river. The last two times they had crossed in a boat. They could go north on the banks until they found a fishing village or some

NPCs, but Mikayla had no idea where the nearest village was and they couldn't afford to waste time.

Even here, where the river was at its thinnest, Mikayla didn't think they would be able to swim across. Suzanne had been nervous about trying to swim the river earlier, and Mikayla didn't know half as much about Io as Suzanne did.

"Any thoughts?" Mikayla asked, gesturing toward the vast river.

"We could set up a zip line," Brit said.

"Really? How do we do that?"

Brit shrugged. "I don't know, with an Archer or something?

"What do you think Suzanne would do?"

"Flirt with an NPC," Brit said. "Seduce him for passage."

Mikayla burst out laughing. "I cannot believe you just said that."

"Yeah," Brit chuckled, "but she had it—"

Her last words were cut off by an eruption in the river. That's what it looked like anyway, as the water bubbled and then exploded as something huge leapt up onto the bank, drenching both girls. It was like the water down by The Floating Eye, both wet and dry at once. Mikayla rubbed her eyes clear and then jumped back in surprise at what was sitting in front of her.

What had caused the inundation was a frog. A rather large frog, about the size of a minivan. Its skin was a bright shade of green, the same color as skunka venom. It regarded Brit and Mikayla with baleful, yellow eyes before opening its mouth to let out a croak. Mikayla saw multiple rows of teeth inside its cavernous maw.

The frog hopped backwards, landing twenty feet away from them. It inhaled air, inflating its throat until the skin bulged translucent. Then it let out a thunderous croak, enough that Mikayla had to take a few steps backwards.

The frog stood up on its hind legs. A small red crown twirled lazily over its head.

"Is this thing a boss?" Brit's voice was full of amazement.

Mikayla put her hands on her hips. "You'd think Suzanne would have told us."

The frog croaked again. In a voice like belching, it said, "What do a pair of puny dry-lubbers want with the Lord of Lily Pads?"

"Oh great," Brit said, equipping her halberd. "The frog can talk."

Mikayla drew her swords. "Well then, let's shut it up."

The Lord of Lily Pads's mouth snapped open. Out flew its tongue like a bullwhip, faster than Mikayla could dodge. She felt something heavy and sticky smash into her left hand, sending one of her swords flying.

The tongue snapped back into the frog's mouth. Mikayla could have sworn the boss was smirking at her.

She saw its jaw snap open again, but this time she was ready. As the tongue flew at her again, she stepped to the side and slashed with her remaining blade. She didn't do a lot of damage, but she slowed the recoil enough that Brit could take a good hack at things.

Two-handed, Brit brought her halberd down. The tongue flopped to the ground, separated from the frog king croaking in agony.

Mikayla jumped forward, the tip of her blade seeking green. She sliced through the Lord of Lily Pads's slimy flesh. The frog threw a webbed punch, but Brit was there to catch the blow on the shaft of her weapon. Mikayla stabbed the creature again.

The Lord of Lily Pads hopped back out of range of the girls. Then, its throat bulged again. Mikayla braced herself for another belch, but wasn't ready for the mouthful of slime spat out.

But Brit was. She shoved Mikayla out of the way. When Mikayla picked herself up off the ground, she saw that Brit was covered in a mucoid layer of gunk.

Mikayla couldn't help herself. "Now you see what I'm talking about," she said.

Brit looked at her hands. She looked up at the Lord of Lily Pads.

Mikayla wasn't sure if it was possible, but now the boss looked afraid.

Brit ran forward, drawing another halberd from her inventory. The Lord of Lily Pads raised its spindly arms to protect itself, but the halberd clove straight through. The monster fell forward and let out one last croak as Brit brought her halberd down on its head.

As the Lord of Lily Pads became pixels, Brit turned to Mikayla. Mikayla did her best not to laugh.

"What the hell is wrong with Suzanne?" Brit asked. "Why would she do this to us?"

Mikayla walked up to her and brushed some slime out of her hair. "Thanks for saving me," she said.

Brit blushed. "I just didn't want to listen to you complain again," she muttered.

The water began to roil again. Fearing more

frogs, Mikayla ran over to retrieve her sword. But it was simply their reward for beating the boss. A series of lily pads bobbed up to the surface, linking one bank of the Ion River to another.

Mikayla took a tentative step onto the first pad. But the pad held her weight fine, and so she took another step and another and before she knew it she was across the Ion River.

Brit came soon after. As soon as she was fully on the bank, the lily pad bridge sank beneath the water.

Mikayla exhaled. Whatever worries she had about Ramses sending his army after them evaporated. Now, her concern for Suzanne could come full to the front. But she remembered what Brit had said, and she fought to control her anxiety. They were in Pyxis now, and for better or for worse, they'd be at the court of New Pyxia soon.

Chapter 5

Brit rolled over and muttered in her sleep. Mikayla looked at her, half in shadow, half in light. Mikayla had never seen anyone else, NPC or player character, move or make noise while sleeping in the game. But, in a way, that made sense: there was no one else like Brit.

After some discussion, they decided that there would probably be fewer monsters near a dead boss, so they camped just a short distance away from the Ion River, opposite the spot where the Lord of Lily Pads had croaked. Brit took the first watch, waking Mikayla up halfway through the night. Since then Mikayla hadn't been watching the surrounding woods as much as she'd watched Brit. In the morning, she didn't make any mention of what she had seen.

They went west with the sun at their backs toward New Pyxia. When they had last left the country, New Pyxia was just an idea of Leo's. He wanted to build a new capital for Pyxis where the ruins of the old capital had stood. Despite her anxiety, Mikayla was excited to see what the Pyxians had accomplished.

The terrain of Pyxis was as rugged as ever—the rocky earth rising and falling over countless hillocks. There were a few small towns which they avoided to save time. They traveled in silence, but Mikayla noticed this was different than the sullen quiet of the days before. Now they were moving with a quiet determination, not wanting to waste their breath on words when they were so close to their destination.

It was as if the game could sense their determination, keeping the monsters well out of their way.

Mikayla saw prides of mountain ligers—huge feral cats with razor-sharp onyx claws—but they seemed content to observe the girls from a distance. Cresting one of the hills they stumbled on a nest of insect-like Reavers. Mikayla drew her swords, but the Reavers buzzed away.

"I don't like this," Brit said. She stood on the broken Reaver nest, watching their retreat. "It's too easy. What's up with all these monsters?"

"Didn't you tell me I needed to lighten up?" Mikayla asked. "Besides, our levels are way higher than theirs. They're probably just scared."

Brit shook her head, but didn't push the point any further. Mikayla wondered if she was disappointed that they didn't have to hack their way through the countryside.

At the top of the next hill Mikayla caught her first sight of New Pyxia. In the past few weeks she had been at both the old and new Capitals of Altair. Both were impressive in their own right: the ebony towers of Fenhold were like a grim shadow in the swamp, while Zenith City dominated the sky around it for miles. New Pyxia was not as forbidding as Fenhold or as much a spectacle as the pillars of Zenith City, but Leo's capital still took her breath away.

While New Pyxia wasn't as tall as the Altairi cities, it covered far more ground. If you took Zenith City and stapled its suburbs to its side then it would approach the area of New Pyxia. It filled the horizon, stretching on and on without end. Mikayla couldn't imagine how the NPCs could have possibly built something so huge in such a short amount of time.

When they reached the following hilltop, Mikayla could see New Pyxia better. From her new vantage she could see that the vast perimeter was merely a wall, and that the city itself lay within. Guard towers were spread along the wall, connected by walkways that ran on top of the barrier. Mikayla's stomach sunk, thinking of all the NPCs they would have to get through if their reception was less than friendly.

"How the hell did they make that?" Brit asked Mikayla. "It's been, what?—a month since we were in Pyxis? There's no way they had the time."

"Maybe Leo had an army working on it."

"Just one?"

"If they didn't sleep." That wasn't much of an explanation, but neither of them had a better idea. Mikayla wished Suzanne was with them to explain it all. She'd know how the NPCs had done it, or would have at least had a good idea. But thinking about Suzanne made Mikayla feel a pang of guilt, again, for leaving her in the Fens.

"Come on," she said to Brit. "We can make it there by sundown."

The rest of the day fell into a pattern. At the top of each hill, New Pyxia's wall reappeared, larger and larger. Then the city would drop from sight as the girls dipped into a valley, only to show up again as they reached the next summit. The monsters they saw still kept a wide distance. Mikayla tried to pay them no mind. Still, their presence made her anxious.

In one of the valleys, they passed within projectile range of a kobold gang. The reptilians watched them pass with unblinking eyes, making Mikayla feel like she had just intruded on a private scene. She hurried on past them, uncomfortable under their stare. The monsters were supposed to attack and loot, not watch her.

When they reached the final hilltop, they stopped and surveyed the city before them. The sun was in front of them now, casting a long shadow from New Pyxia's wall. The whole city was made of alabaster stone, and it caught the technicolor sunset, glowing with brilliant light.

Mikayla distinguished the shops and inns that populated the outskirts of the city, no doubt filled with merchants and travelers. Further in were mansions and small towers: the homes of the rich and influential NPCs. At the city's southern edge sat a huge coliseum, much like Zenith City's. It looked empty to Mikayla, a husk waiting for entertainment to fill it.

Small domed buildings sprang up regularly within the city. These were the Oratoriums, the Pyxians' tributes to their departed. Mikayla had only briefly gone into the Oratorium at Vale, but the rows of statues it housed, memorializing dead NPCs, impressed and intimidated her.

Yet, what truly caught her eye, as she regarded New Pyxia, were the canals. The whole of the city was crisscrossed by canals of water, glittering like liquid gold in the sunset. Mikayla spotted NPCs poling gondolas up and down the canals, transporting other NPCs and piles of weapons between the city blocks.

Tracing the golden canals through New Pyxia led to a lake in the center of the city. Drawbridges over the lake led to an island. Built on the island was a domed structure, like an Oratorium, but several times the size.

As she stared at the resplendent waters lapping at that alabaster shore, Mikayla could only think, *It's beautiful.* After spending so much time in the Fens and on the move, she had forgotten how breathtaking Io could be.

"Damn," Brit whispered. She was looking straight ahead, a smile spreading across her lips. Despite their arguing over these past few days, despite Mikayla's uncertainty about Leo, despite how worried she was about Suzanne, despite everything, Mikayla was happy to be here with Brit. As they stood on the hill overlooking New Pyxia, the virtual world was at peace. *If only it could always be like this*, Mikayla thought. *Maybe we wouldn't have to leave.* It was a silly notion, she knew that, but something told her that if she said it to Brit right now, Brit wouldn't disagree.

Before she could make any confessions, Io reasserted itself. The NPCs on the wall lifted the gate as a platoon raced out of the city and across the countryside toward the girls. There were at least twenty of them, all armed and armored.

"Company," Mikayla said. Brit shrugged, having already seen.

If they're Pyxians then we should have nothing to worry about. After all, Brit and Mikayla had both fought for Pyxis on The Floating Eye and in the war before that. She wasn't expecting a hero's welcome, but she thought they had earned better than an armed response.

"Let's meet them halfway," Brit said, breaking into a jog. Mikayla followed her down the hill and onto the plain. Blades of wild grass snipped at her knees, her swords rattling in their sheathes as she ran to catch up.

The Pyxians split into two groups as they

approached the girls, closing in on them in a pincer. Their weapons were all drawn, Mikayla noted. Most of the NPCs were Fighters, Monks, and Archers, but there were Swiftblades, like Mikayla, and a few more characters in advanced classes. It was a group balanced between melee and ranged characters, bulky and nimble. In short, exactly what you would want to send out to meet an enemy.

But we aren't enemies. Despite having spent so much time with the Pyxian Army, Mikayla didn't recognize a single face in the circle.

One of the Swiftblades stepped forward. He was tall and slender, like his class would suggest, with pale green eyes and his long brown hair tied up in a topknot. Mikayla could feel his eyes searching her, analyzing her character for weakness. Out of all the Pyxians, only his weapon remained undrawn. He walked toward the girls with the cool confidence of a commander. He didn't shout but still spoke firmly. "State your purpose here."

"We're here to see Leo," Brit responded. She towered over the Pyxian, but the Pyxians had them outnumbered ten to one.

"Do you mean the king?" he asked scornfully.

"Are there any other Leos?" Brit replied. Mikayla could have kicked her. This was exactly the wrong way to have this conversation.

"What business do you have with the king?" the Swiftblade asked.

"We seek an audience with King Leo," Mikayla said. She could practically hear Brit rolling her eyes; Brit always made fun of her for talking like that with NPCs, but her prettified speech worked.

The Swiftblade turned from Brit to Mikayla, and in a more polite tone, said, "My king is very busy with the concerns of his kingdom. If you tell me why you seek this audience I can relay the message."

"Listen," Brit said, before Mikayla could stop her. "You see that nice city down there? You wouldn't have if it wasn't for us. If it wasn't for us, you'd all be stuck with Ramses for a king, okay?"

The next thing Mikayla knew Brit had grabbed her and was holding her up for display. "We're two of the Pyxian champions from The Floating Eye. So you can either take us to Leo, or you can get the fuck out of our way."

Smooth, Mikayla thought as the Pyxians closed in around them. But the Swiftblade raised his hand, stopping their approach. He was staring at the two of them like he had just seen them for the first time.

"Put me down," Mikayla hissed. Brit complied, immediately dropping her. Mikayla landed lightly on her feet.

"Lady Brit?" he asked. "And you would be Lady Mikayla?"

"I don't know about the lady part," Brit said. "But I'm pretty sure I'm the only Brit in Io, and Mikayla here is definitely one of a kind."

"My deepest apologies," the Swiftblade said,

touching a hand to his forehead and bowing at the waist. "My name is Elias, a humble soldier of Pyxis. I did not recognize the two of you. Please, follow me into the city. You are too late to see the king today, but I will take you to him first thing in the morning."

The rest of the Pyxians fell into a formation around the two of them. When Mikayla asked the Swiftblade about it, he said it was for protection.

Whose protection? Mikayla wondered. *Ours or the city's?*

Chapter 6

It had been two days since Ramses paid his little visit, and Crux hadn't come back to see her once. Suzanne felt a little foolish for missing the Dragoon, but his company was better than nothing. She found herself looking forward to the jailers' check-ins now, so starved was she for contact.

Her isolation left her with plenty of time to think. Would Ramses actually kill her? Suzanne had thought she was safe. In the early days of testing Io, she had died plenty of times. But that was before she was playing with the TII, back when the world was viewed through a computer screen and not lived, like she was living it now. Death through a computer screen was meaningless.

She had died thousands of times in other games. Whether missing a platform and falling on spikes, failing to block a fifteen-hit combo or simply driving a car off a bridge out of boredom, death was relatively meaningless. Like in any FPS when playing online. You died, the screen went red for a second, and then you respawned somewhere else, with your starting gun and your health bar restored. Death was a loading screen in those games.

And in Io, it had been much the same. Like any RPG, once dead you had to restore your game from your last save. As soon as Suzanne added in the autosave function death became pretty much the same as in a shooter—die and respawn at an earlier point in the dungeon.

Yet it wasn't exactly the same. When she died, or when Brit or Mikayla died in testing, they were logged out of the game. The return to reality was jarring but only temporary. When they logged back in, though, Io was always different than how they had left it. Even the deaths of the player characters didn't stop Io from running. And Brit had convinced Suzanne to change the way death worked in the game: to make it permanent, even for the player characters. Suzanne had agreed, wanting to make the game harder. Now, if a character died in Io, they were gone for good.

Suzanne had often wondered if dying was just the answer. It would be so simple to let her health points drop to zero. But she couldn't do it. She couldn't shake the fear that dying would trap her in some kind of limbo between worlds, unable to return to reality but unable to log back in. Maybe it was her natural instinct for self-preservation. Now that they weren't just playing Io, but living it, she felt more intensely linked with her avatar.

She didn't want to die. Brit and Mikayla were counting on her to find some way back to reality. Her dad was counting on her, too. She didn't want to have her character die here and be gone from the real world forever. She had already seen that happen to her father once, losing someone he loved. Suzanne didn't want that to happen to him again.

Freedom was the first step. Once she was out of the cell, she could go from there. All that meant was that she had to convince Crux. She had to make him see sense.

She heard a commotion coming from beneath her. For a while, Suzanne suspected she was being kept in Fenhold's tower, away from any other potential prisoners. But now there was clearly a ruckus going on nearby. She heard muted shouts and the clash of weapons. The noise grew louder.

Then, the next thing she knew, Porter the Sellsword flew past her cell. She heard a crash as he smashed into a wall. She didn't hear him get up.

Suzanne stood up, holding her hands in front of her. She didn't know what was coming, but she was as ready as she could be for a fight.

But it didn't come to that. Crux stuck his head in front of her cell.

"Hello," he said. "I did a lot of thinking. I think you are right and I should set you free."

Suzanne was too dumbfounded to say anything. Crux didn't need any instruction from her. He wrapped a massive hand around two of the bars and pulled. With a grunt and a screech of metal the bars came loose in his hands, pixelating as he let them fall.

The Dragoon ducked into her cell. He knelt by the iron rung, through which her shackles ran, and yanked it free of the floor. He ripped her chain into two like it was made of paper. Suzanne couldn't have picked the shackles off her wrists, but thanks to Crux, they too turned into pixels.

And just like that, she was free.

"Crux," she said, "thank you."

The Dragoon gave her a dopey smile. "Now we have to find Burgrave!" he said.

"No," Suzanne said. "First, we have to get out of here."

Suzanne looked out a window for the first time since her captivity began and saw it was night. Io's moon was full in the sky, illuminating the Fens. She remembered a similar view the night she was captured. Even though it was still a game, Suzanne couldn't help being a little mesmerized by the moon. Soon she would be out of this castle of cold stone and on her way to find her friends.

It had been a week since she first came to Fenhold. Suzanne hadn't explored a ton of the castle, but Crux was an able guide. She told him to steer them well clear of Ramses's chambers, where there was a trapdoor down to the subterranean tunnels. She had just regained her freedom and wasn't particularly eager to run back into Xenos. As they tiptoed through the castle, Suzanne flipped through her Menu and formed a party with Crux. That would make healing go faster and limit the friendly fire they could do to each other in fights.

Suzanne was far more interested in limiting the damage Crux could do to her. After seeing what he did to her chains, she wasn't going to take any risks.

The hallways were completely empty. She realized that the summit must have ended while she was a prisoner. Maybe it broke up because she disappeared. Still, she moved slowly, sticking to the shadows. It never hurt to be too careful.

But Fenhold was silent. Not the silence of sleeping NPCs. No, the castle was absolutely silent. No NPCs stood guard. Their footsteps echoed loudly down the hallways, but no other footsteps echoed back. The silence unsettled Suzanne. She had only heard Io devoid of sound like this once before: in the tunnels beneath Fenhold, when she had found Xenos and Ramses.

"Where is everyone?" Suzanne whispered.

"I do not know," Crux replied. He looked scared.

But despite her nerves, nothing jumped out at them. They walked through the cavernous halls of Fenhold, coming out into the castle's northern courtyard. Suzanne drew her daggers, ready for a fight, but the courtyard was empty and there were no guards on the walls.

Half of her wanted to investigate this, but she knew the wiser course of action would be to put as much distance between herself and the castle while she still could.

"Let's go," she whispered. They crossed into the moonlit courtyard. Then Suzanne heard pounding footsteps behind them. Finally, the guards had shown up for a fight. Suzanne almost grinned. She had a lot of pent-up aggression to let out.

But it was only one NPC: Ramses.

The king's face was a mask of terror. He didn't seem to register that it Suzanne and Crux in the courtyard. Before Suzanne could stop him, the king bolted past her, running full tilt through the gates and out into the Fens. He disappeared between the swamp trees.

"What the fuck?" Suzanne said.

"My king . . . " Crux frowned. "No. Not my king. No longer."

As happy as Suzanne was to hear that, Crux's declaration didn't explain where Ramses was going. She heard more footsteps and motioned for Crux to stand out of the way of the doors.

A dozen NPCs, as scared as Ramses, stampeded out of the castle. Suzanne recognized them as members of Ramses's court, some dating as far back as his Zenith City days. All of the NPCs belonged to the Citizen class. They were running away from whatever was in the castle as fast as they could.

Bringing up the rear of the NPCs was a sturdy Citizen decked out in a brilliant blue cape. Suzanne found herself unable to take her eyes off the cape for some reason. That was where she first noticed it. The cape began to lose its color and its flexibility. As she watched, it became rigid and gray, like it was made of stone. The grayness spread along the cape, traveling up to the NPC.

And then the NPC began to gray as well. First his shoulders hardened, then his arms, and up his neck to his head. His face was frozen in a strangled scream. The untouched legs carried the statuesque torso a few steps forward before they too grayed and became still.

Then the next NPC turned, and then the next. One by one they transformed until the courtyard wasn't filled with NPCs, but statues. Suzanne walked over to the caped statue and touched it. It felt coarse to her touch. The statue wobbled and fell, banging against the cobblestone courtyard. But the statue didn't break.

The stricken expression on the statues proved too much for Suzanne. "Come on," she said, grabbing Crux's hand. He hadn't turned into a statue like the others, for which Suzanne felt profoundly grateful. Half-leading, half-pulling, she managed to get Crux through the main gate of Fenhold.

"I knew them," he said. "They lived in the castle with me."

Suzanne wanted to comfort the giant, but she didn't know what to say.

"I do not think they will be okay," Crux added.

The Fens never let travelers pass easily. The first time Suzanne had traveled through them, she had regretted programming them, but now they were downright terrifying. The cries of Screechers echoed through the canopy. Suzanne was already jumpy, and each shrill cry ratcheted her anxiety up another notch.

But at least there was noise in the swamp. She shuddered, remembering the uncanny stillness of the castle and the courtyard. She had no idea what had caused the NPCs' transformation, but she didn't plan to stick around long enough to find out.

Crux had a hard time getting through the Fens. Suzanne remembered Brit having similar difficulties, which made sense as they were both Dragoons. They kept stopping to pull Crux up out of the muck whenever he sank in.

Finally, they came to a part of the Fens where the canopy was thin and the moonlight shone through. Wearily, Crux sat down on a log, which cracked under his bulk but didn't break all the way. Suzanne looked around anxiously, ready to keep moving.

"I'll look ahead," she said. Crux nodded. He hadn't spoken a word since they entered the Fens. Suzanne wondered if he would speak again.

She could move much more quickly without Crux. Slicing through several vines, she found a firm path where it would be easier going for the Dragoon. She was about to turn back and fetch him when she heard a laugh.

She froze, unsure if it was just a trick of the Fens. But then she heard the laugh again, more clearly. Suzanne crept forward. Peering around a tree, she saw Ramses, the king of Altair, sitting on a log.

His boots were stained with muck. Somewhere in the Fens he had lost his crown, and his gray curls hung wildly around his manic eyes.

Suzanne stayed hidden behind the tree, but Ramses wouldn't have noticed her. He was fully absorbed by his hand, which had just begun to turn gray. The king shook his head and laughed again.

"What did you do?" Suzanne asked, stepping out from her hiding place. Ramses looked up at her with what could only be disappointment.

"You mean it hasn't affected you? Damn that Xenos! He promised to protect me, and he protects you? What the hell is he playing at?"

"Xenos did this?" Once more, Suzanne was awed by the NPC's power.

Ramses sneered at her. "Who else could have? When I found him in the Oracle Chamber I should have never let him out. He's been even more trouble than you and your obnoxious little friends."

"What do you mean *let him out*? How did you even get into the Oracle Chamber in the first place?"

Ramses gave her a sardonic look. "I had a key."

By then the gray had spread to his wrist and forearm.

"What a pity," Ramses sighed, "to think that the great Ramses, the king of Altair, would come to his end in a swamp, undone by his own servant. And only Suzanne to keep him company. I think a king deserves better than this."

Suzanne had a hundred questions she wanted to ask Ramses, but she could see that he was beyond responding. At least there was one thing she could get from him. She drew her dagger and took a step forward.

"Oh, oh, oh," Ramses cackled. "Finally taking your so-called revenge, I see. Well, do what you must. If it gives you pleasure to kill the evil king who tormented you then I will not stop you. I cannot stop you."

"And besides," he said, holding up his arm. It was now gray up to the bicep. "I haven't much time anyway. Best kill the king while you can."

"You aren't a king," Suzanne said. She grabbed him by the shoulder and shoved him forward onto the blade of her dagger. He gasped in pain.

"You're nothing," she said. "You're less than nothing. You're a bad memory. As soon as I get out of this game, every trace of you will be deleted forever."

Ramses opened his mouth to reply, but no words came out. His body began to pixelate, even as the graying continued, so that by the time he had dispersed into pixels his entire arm and part of his shoulder remained as gray stone.

When Suzanne led Crux through that way shortly after, the stone had sunk into the Fens. There was nothing there.

Chapter 7

"Don't rock the boat!" the NPC gondolier shouted. Brit sat up, shaking the boat even more as she did so. It wasn't her fault that the Pyxians didn't have a gondola big enough for her. She had wanted to walk anyway, but that Swiftblade, Elias, told her that would be impossible.

"The only way into Castle Pyxia now is by boat," he explained. "And we will have to hurry if we wish to make it in at all today."

So Brit had squeezed herself into the gondola. Her knees were pressed up against her chest and every time she tried to adjust her seat to get more comfortable, the boat shook.

"Do you want us to fall out?" Elias asked. If Brit didn't know better, she would have thought he was trying to make a joke. Even if they did fall out, the canal was shallow enough that they could all stand. And besides, the canals were so clogged with water traffic Brit would fall into another boat if she went overboard.

The same traffic meant the journey was taking forever. They had set out early in the morning, and it looked like they wouldn't be reaching the castle until sunset. Brit was getting antsy just thinking about spending so long in the glorified canoe.

"Try to sit still," Mikayla said. *Easy for her to say,* Brit thought. Mikayla's character fit in the boat. She had spent their gondola ride speaking with Elias while Brit squirmed in her seat and tried to memorize the path the gondola took through the canals. There was always a full moon in Io, and between moonlight and the numerous torches lit along the city streets, Brit could see almost as well as she could during the day.

Plenty of Pyxians lined the streets that ran alongside and the bridges that crossed over the canals. Merchants hocked goods—not just weapons and armor, but foods and furniture. The gondola poled past a street corner where Brit could've sworn she saw two NPCs haggling over the price of a pet weremonkey, but they moved on before she could get a second look.

The Pyxians wore the same flowing robes that Brit remembered, yet these robes were fringed with golden thread and embroidered with intricate designs. She couldn't recall Libra or any of her subjects ever dressing so elegantly. More than anything else, the newfound foppery reminded her of the upper-crust of Zenith City.

Elias prattled on and on about the various amenities the city provided, sounding just like a tour guide on a field trip. Thinking back on those bussed excursions, Brit remembered that the best part (besides leaving school for the day and breaking the routine monotony of classes) was sneaking off from the tour and really exploring the place. Trapped in the gondola, she was submitted to Elias' dissertation, without the ability to check facts herself. She longed to get into the shadows of New Pyxia and see what it was really like. But they were on a mission, she reminded herself, and the sooner they got to Leo, the sooner they could convince him to help rescue Suzanne.

Even if she felt like making a break for it—and she wouldn't, because Mikayla would never let her hear the end of it—Brit doubted she could get away from their escorts. Her gondola contained her, Mikayla, Elias, and the NPC propelling the boat, but they were preceded and followed by two boats full of Pyxian warriors.

The buildings lining the sides of the canal grew shorter, and the narrow waterway deepened as it led out into a lake. On the opposite shore, Brit could see more city blocks, but the NPC poling them along steered the gondola for the lake's center. There lay Castle Pyxia, Leo's new home.

Leo couldn't have built himself a better moat. If New Pyxia ever came under attack, Brit imagined that the king's keep would be impossible to take. It was just like Leo to plan for war when they were at peace.

As they neared the huge dome that was Castle Pyxia, Brit could see dozens of windows curved into the top of the dome. But besides those openings, the castle was perfectly hemispherical. With the setting sun's glow fully on it, Castle Pyxia almost looked like a celestial body itself.

Brit couldn't see a dock or anywhere to disembark from the boat. But then she saw a rocky island rising up out of the lake, maybe fifty yards from Castle Pyxia. That was where the gondolier aimed them.

They exited the gondola onto a jetty made of the same white stone as the immense dome. A thin drawbridge connected the jetty to the Castle proper.

"If you would follow me," Elias said, stepping

quickly to the front. The drawbridge was so narrow they had to go single file. Elias took the lead followed by several guards, then Mikayla, and then Brit, with another set of guards bringing up the rear.

"I think it's safe to say Leo wasn't expecting visitors," Brit muttered.

Mikayla nodded toward Elias. Brit caught her meaning: he was a Swiftblade, like Mikayla, which meant he had probably heard that. But if he did, Elias gave no sign, simply leading them back around the island to the front of the dome. In some ways Elias struck her as Leo's response to Burgrave. He certainly had the attitude down right.

When Elias stopped, it took Brit a moment to realize they were in front of a set of towering doors. Whoever had made them had cunningly carved them right from the dome itself, leaving only a hairline crack to indicate that this was a way out. Elias knocked on the marble three times and took a step back.

Noiselessly, the doors glided open.

The interior of the castle was dimly lit between the scattered torches and the light trickling in from the high windows. Once Brit's eyes adjusted, she could see that it truly was a dome. Narrow stairs wrapped around the interior, leading to catwalks and suspended platforms. There were no walls within the castle. Instead, heavy curtains divided each floor into rooms.

"It is late," Elias said. "And the king has already retired for the evening. I will show you to your rooms, and tomorrow you will have your audience."

Brit would have argued if Elias had stayed around long enough to listen. He immediately set off up one of the winding stairs. Brit and Mikayla exchanged a look and followed after him. Brit was almost surprised when the guards didn't ascend the stairs behind them.

The narrow stairs were built out from the wall of the dome, so they didn't wobble or even creak. Still, would it have killed Leo to put a handrail in? Brit wasn't afraid of heights, but you'd have to be an idiot not to feel queasy climbing the stone steps. She didn't want to look weak in front of the Pyxians so she ignored the shaking in her knees and pressed on, higher and higher up the stairs.

After passing two of the suspended platforms they were near the top of the dome. Elias led them down a suspended walkway to the third platform. Like the ground level, it was divided by curtains, these ones hanging from the roof of the dome. The hangings formed a corridor: walking down it they became a pair of pulled back drapes. Inside the room were two beds, an end table, and everything else the girls had come used to seeing in the inns and guest rooms of Io.

"Until morning," Elias said, making the same gesture of touching his forehead and bowing before padding off back down the steps.

Brit flopped on her bed. She unequipped her armor, falling the half-inch once it disappeared from her body back into her inventory. Mikayla always stood to take her armor off, like it was clothing and not just an element of the game. Once her armor was off, Mikayla crossed the room and closed the curtain opening.

"Do you think he'll help us?" she asked, still facing the curtains.

"I don't know," Brit said. "I think the real question is, will he help Suzanne?"

Mikayla didn't answer her. She walked back to her bed and dropped onto it, letting the game put her to sleep. Brit watched Mikayla until sleep took her as well.

That night, she dreamed she was wrapped in one of the castle's curtains. "I'm the Queen of Pyxis!" she shouted, parading around in her fake gown. Mikayla was there, laughing along. Then the curtain became heavier, dragging Brit down. She tried to stand up, and realized she was falling.

The curtains will catch me, she thought, but then she was lying on the ground again. She tried to get up, but someone dropped another curtain on her. Another, and then another. She felt herself getting crushed beneath their weight, but there was nothing she could do.

"Oh Brit," she heard Mikayla say. "Won't you ever—" and then she woke up.

Sunlight poured in through the windows above them. Brit inhaled and exhaled. It had just been a dream. Looking over at Mikayla's bed, she saw Mikayla was still asleep. Brit thought about waking her and telling her about the dream. It had been one of her tamer dreams, one that probably wouldn't scare Mikayla. Brit didn't know what she would say if Mikayla asked about her other dreams. Maybe she could lie and say this was the first one? But Brit didn't want to lie to Mikayla about her dreams or anything else. She didn't want to keep hiding how she felt.

Regardless, it still didn't feel like an appropriate time to talk about the dreams. Right now they had to focus on Suzanne. Brit rolled on to her other side and pretended to be asleep when Mikayla woke up, letting Mikayla get dressed and shake her before stirring.

Brit led the way down the stairs, steadying herself with a hand on the wall of the dome. In the daylight, the inside of Castle Pyxia glowed alabaster. Many of the curtains were pulled back, revealing apartments like the one they were staying in.

On the ground floor, all the curtains had been pulled to the side. Where there had been apartments the night before, there was now an audience chamber the size of the castle's interior. Seated on a throne, on the opposite of the dome from the entrance—the literal length of the island away—was Leo, king of Pyxis.

"Hey!" Brit shouted, waving. She figured going in friendly was the best approach. After all, she and Leo had fought side by side while defending Vale in the war between Pyxis and Altair and as champions of Pyxis on The Floating Eye.

Rows of Citizens sat on backless chairs. They were dressed in the same finery Brit had seen among the more prominent merchants on the canals. They flanked the dais seating Leo and his attendants. Some of the guards from the day before stood at attention behind the dais. Brit searched the faces of the NPCs present for Rigel, Mallon, and Alphonse, the NPCs who had fought alongside them for Pyxis. But they were nowhere to be seen.

Brit was halfway to Leo and he still hadn't returned her greeting. An NPC stepped forward and in a loud voice proclaimed, "The Ladies Brit and Mikayla, heroes of Pyxis, champions of The Floating Eye!"

In unison, the Citizens rose and all made the same bowing gesture that Elias had the day before.

The NPCs on the dais rose as well and likewise bowed. Leo rose last, smiling to greet them, but what Brit noticed first was his crown. The crown had gemstones embedded all the way around it. They pulsed green, revealing themselves to be Energite. Libra never wore a crown like this. *And Libra never sat on a throne,* Brit realized.

On top of his Pyxian robe, Leo wore a heavy vermilion cape that clashed terribly with his sandy hair. He looked less like a king and more like a clown. Brit glanced over at Mikayla to see how she was handling it, but Mikayla was staring straight at the edge of the dais. Brit followed her gaze and stopped in her tracks from the shock.

Sitting at the end of the dais, bowing along with the rest of the nobles, was Xenos.

Chapter 8

As soon as she entered New Pyxia, Mikayla started feeling uneasy. Over the next day, she did her best to feign interest while Elias delivered his never-ending lecture on the city, smiling and nodding while the Swiftblade waxed romantic on every canal, bridge, and street corner. Mikayla never felt at ease while traveling by water in Io, but this was something else entirely.

Libra, Leo's older sister and the ruler of Pyxis before him, had asked Mikayla to be her successor. Perhaps that was part of Mikayla's discomfort as she gazed down the streets and canals of New

Pyxia. She wondered if she was assessing everything, wondering how she would have run things if she had followed Libra's dying wish. Mikayla couldn't imagine constructing anything so grand.

But all her wonder came crashing down when she saw Xenos on the dais.

The NPC had his hood pulled down over his face as usual, but there was no mistaking Xenos. His cloak was the same: deep purple with a gold design snaking its way around the arms. In all of Io, Mikayla had never seen another NPC wear anything like it. But more than the clothes, just looking at Xenos made her feel uneasy, like she was on the verge of remembering something unpleasant she had forgotten. What could he possibly be doing here?

Mikayla felt like running and attacking Xenos. Before she could do either, Leo was striding toward her and Brit with his arms spread wide.

"Brit!" he exclaimed. "Mikayla! It's so good to see you again. Is Suzanne with you?"

Mikayla looked from the beaming Leo to Xenos and back to the king. In her shock at seeing Xenos, she had only glanced at Leo. Up close, she could see he looked ridiculous. Even in a world filled with armored NPCs and fantastic monsters, the king of Pyxis looked like a doofus. His crown was so big that his neck seemed to be on the verge of collapsing under it. Over his robe, he wore a violently red cape.

But there were important things to talk about than Leo's lack of fashion sense. As always, Mikayla could count on Brit to bypass the bullshit.

"What the fuck is he doing here?" Brit nearly shouted, pointing a finger at Xenos.

Leo took a step back as if he'd been hit. The heads of all the attendant NPCs swiveled from the three of them to Xenos.

The king's smile slipped for a moment but reappeared right after. "Xenos is one of my chief advisors. Now, as I was saying, when should we expect Suzanne?"

"What do you mean he's one of your chief advisors?" Mikayla demanded. "You know he was one Ramses's champions on The Floating Eye, right? You remember that he beat you?"

Whispers broke out among the attendees. Leo, his anger beginning to show, beckoned to Elias, who in turn signaled to guards stationed beside the citizenry. At once, the guards began to usher the Citizens out. On cue, the NPCs on the dais besides Xenos exited as well.

When they were gone, leaving Brit and Mikayla, Xenos, and Leo, the king said, "I'll thank you not to remind me of my failures. After The Floating Eye and the disgraceful actions of Ramses, Xenos came to me. He said he was blind to Ramses's true nature and begged for my forgiveness."

"You just trusted him like that?" Mikayla couldn't believe what she was hearing. Leo, who hated everything to do with Altair, just forgave one of the Altairi champions?

"I chose to trust him and he has repaid that trust a thousandfold," the king sniffed.

"Bullshit," Brit said.

"I assure you," Xenos replied, rising, his voice icy. "I have seen the error of my ways. The king has chosen to forgive me. Would you have him censure all who once served Ramses? Then how could he trust you?"

"That's completely different!" Mikayla was finding it hard not to shout. "And it's besides the point! Xenos still works for Ramses! We saw him at the summit at Fenhold!"

"What are you talking about?" Leo replied, amazed. "Xenos has been with me since we began the construction of New Pyxia. He hardly had time to go traipsing through the Fens."

"Bullshit!" Brit yelled again. "We saw him there. Where's Rigel? He was there too! You can ask him if you don't believe us."

"Rigel is with Alphonse and Lynx in Vale," Leo

said. "They guard the north of Pyxis against potential invasion."

Everything she heard made Mikayla feel less and less comfortable with what Leo was saying. She was worried when she hadn't seen Rigel or Alphonse or any of the old guard in New Pyxia, but she had hoped that they were just out on missions and would be at the Capital soon. But based on what Leo was saying, the only advice the king got in New Pyxia was coming from Xenos.

"Why are you worried about a potential invasion when you've already been invaded?" she asked, staring at Xenos.

"Enough of this nonsense," Leo snapped. "You are guests and friends or else I would not tolerate such behavior. You are overtired from your long journey. Perhaps more rest will restore your senses, and your courtesy. When Suzanne joins us we can speak about this matter further."

"Excuse me?" Mikayla spat back. "We're overtired? Newsflash, Leo—Suzanne isn't coming. You want to know why? Ramses and Xenos took her prisoner in the Fens. That's why we came here in the first place, to get help rescuing her. But obviously you're more interested in playing dress-up and building canals than helping out your friends."

A dazed expression appeared on Leo's face. Mikayla felt a moment of pity for the king. After all, he had probably been waiting for Suzanne to return to Pyxis so he could show her all he had built.

"Suzanne . . . a prisoner?" he asked. He seemed lost, helpless at the revelation, on the verge of collapsing.

"My king," Xenos said, walking down from the dais and grabbing Leo's arm to steady him. At the moment they touched, Mikayla thought she saw the Energite in Leo's crown pulse, but she couldn't be sure.

Xenos walked Leo back up the steps and eased him down into the throne. Mikayla thought it was a bit much—had Leo really been that pressed on Suzanne that news of her capture would knock the wind out of him like this? Suzanne hadn't broken things off in clear terms, but Leo had to have gotten the hint by now, right?

"We must rescue her," the king said weakly.

"No shit," Brit replied. "You said most of the army's at Vale, right? How fast can they get here?"

"Two days' time, if necessary," Leo answered. "But there is no need for them to come here. It will be faster if they head straight for the Fens." His voice grew stronger with each word. Whatever that fainting spell was, it seemed to have passed.

"Is that so wise, my king?" Xenos asked. "Should we not first confirm her location before deploying the army?"

"I bet he knows where Ramses is keeping Suze," Brit said. "Don't you, Xenos? You're just stalling so Ramses has time to move her before we get there."

"I believe King Leo rules Pyxis, not you," Xenos replied. "I merely offer my advice. What would be worse, my king? Delaying until our goal is clear or rushing in blindly and being punished for this girl's impatience? This all assumes that Suzanne has indeed been captured and that this is not all some ploy. If we move our North Guard, we leave Pyxis vulnerable to invasion."

"That is enough, Xenos, and enough on that matter from you as well, Brit," Leo said before she could gloat. "I trust both of you and hope that you can learn to trust each other. For now, if you cannot abide being in each other's presence then you will excuse yourself from the throne room."

Mikayla could see they were losing ground with Leo, so she grabbed Brit's arm to warn her against speaking against Xenos further. Xenos was going to delay them as best he could, even if that meant arguing with them over his loyalty to Leo. Leo wanted to help them, so maybe the move was to get out of his way and let him. "We don't have time to waste," she said. "We need to rescue Suzanne as soon as possible. Every minute we spend debating this is another minute we're leaving her to Ramses."

Leo's brow was furrowed in thought. "I will think on what the right course of action will be and call for you later today," he said.

He rose from his throne again and walked with Mikayla and Brit to the door of his palace. "For today, at least, I hope you can enjoy what New Pyxia has to offer. We will rescue Suzanne, I know it. But we must be cautious. I cannot be the headstrong prince I was."

"That's exactly who we need you to be," Mikayla said. Leo had been uncompromising, nearing on fanatical, but now he was comfortable. He had built his city, built the walls around it, and was now used to sitting on a throne.

Leo shook his head, and Mikayla saw he looked a little sad at her words. "We will rescue her," he repeated. Then he turned around and walked away, the curtains of Castle Pyxia swallowing him.

Chapter 9

The air was as crisp as the leaves lining the roads. Child NPCs took running jumps into the leaf piles, hooting and giggling as they crunched through the leaves. Parents and village elders watched from the stoops of their houses, chatting idly as their children played.

Suzanne watched as well, hidden on a rooftop. The season had changed while Suzanne was captive in the Fens. That should have been impossible, but the evidence was smacking her in the face. Next thing she knew it would be snowing. Seasons were on the short list of features to add to Io, but that had been before she was trapped in the game.

Whatever was fucking with her code must have added them in, but why would they do that? What purpose could such a peaceful autumn afternoon serve?

At least these villagers were alive. Suzanne shuddered remembering the other villages they had come to—rows and rows of NPCs frozen slack-jawed just like the court of Ramses. Suzanne tried to view it as a glitch in the game, the areas becoming corrupted and freezing the NPCs within. But then she would stumble upon a child frozen mid-step and that illusion shattered. Had Xenos passed through all those towns, subjecting the Citizens to the same bizarre half-death? Suzanne wasn't sure what the NPC had done, but whatever it was seemed to be slowing down. They were traveling faster after leaving the Fens, but Suzanne still wasn't sure how they had outrun the gray.

She watched the townsfolk for another minute before deciding that this wasn't a trap. Shimmying backwards on the roof, she dropped down behind the house and stole off into the forest to fetch Crux. She scouted out the villages while he hid to the best of his abilities. Their surroundings hadn't always been able to hide an NPC of his size, but then, none of the previous villages had anyone they needed to hide from.

She found him in the ruins of a leaf pile. Unlike the children, who sent the leaves fluttering upwards upon impact, Crux crashing into the leaf pile dealt the leaves too much damage. He was just too heavy. All around him leaves were pixelating.

Despite that, the giant was smiling ear to ear.

"Suzanne!" he boomed. "We will stop in this village?"

As much as he had annoyed her while they traveled together, Suzanne was happy for Crux's upbeat attitude. She had put off abandoning the NPC, partly because she had become used to his company, and partly because she could use the extra muscle in a fight. If she was right, they'd have to fight a boss to cross the Ion River, and she could certainly use the Dragoon's war hammer when dealing with the Lord of Lily Pads.

"Yeah," she said. "Come on. Let's circle around and come in the main road."

In no time they were at the gates to the village Ostia. Suzanne saw that their appearance earned uneasy looks from the townspeople. The children, oblivious to the threat that advanced-class strangers might pose, were ushered inside. Citizens reached for makeshift weapons.

Maybe I should have come alone, Suzanne thought. Crux received most of the Citizens' wary attentions. And who could blame them? Next to the hulking Dragoon, an Infiltrator was hardly a concern.

Crux didn't help matters by walking right up to the nearest NPC and asking in his booming voice, "Where is Burgrave?"

He got no answer besides a frightened look and a quick retreat inside his home.

Crux looked confused, almost hurt by the NPC

fleeing. "How about I ask the questions?" Suzanne said. *Otherwise we'll be here all day,* she thought.

At the next house, the NPCs had already locked the door. Suzanne knocked—she hoped not too loudly—three times. The door opened half an inch, enough for her to see the mistrustful eye of an NPC.

"Yes?" the NPC asked in a tone anything but polite.

"Good afternoon," Suzanne said, trying to remember how Mikayla did her prettified speech. She was always the best at talking to NPCs. "We're looking for three people. Their names are Burgrave, Brit, and Mikayla. Has anyone under those names passed through your village?"

"Who wants to know?" the NPC replied.

"We're friends of theirs," Suzanne answered.

"If you are such good friends then how come they did not tell you where they were going?" Before Suzanne could reply the door slammed shut in her face.

She stood on the porch of the cottage, unsure of what to do.

"What did they say?" Crux asked.

Suzanne fought the urge to kick him. She had tried to go about this the nice way, but it looked like that option was closed to her. She placed a hand on the doorknob and initiated the lock-picking mini-game. On a random village door like this it was practically child's play. The door swung inwards and Suzanne stepped into the cottage, Crux tromping up the steps behind her.

A projectile flew at her. She snatched it out of the air. It was a makeshift spear, hardly more than a sharp stick. The family that owned the cottage cowered behind a table; a mother, father, and little boy clinging to each other in fear. Suzanne felt a sickening sense of déjà vu. This was just how it had been when she had gone on the first raids of Altair with Leo. The Citizens were just as scared of her then, like she was a villain. Well, that was a part she might have to play.

"Cute," she said, breaking the stick over her knee. "We don't want to hurt you. We're just trying to find our friends, okay? So did they come through here?"

Crux squeezed through the door. "Burgrave is my best friend. He is about this high," he said, holding his hand at his waist. "He does not have much hair. But he is very nice!"

Neither of the adults spoke. The child piped up, "That's not very tall!"

The adults looked mortified as the massive Dragoon approached their child.

"No," Crux replied solemnly. "He is not very tall. But he is a very great man and my friend. We need to find him."

"I . . . I don't know about any Burgraves," the woman said, "but we did get a traveler coming through here a little while back. Short, just like you said."

"What about the other two?" Suzanne asked.

"Brit's big like him," she said, pointing to Crux,

"and Mikayla's a little taller than me. She always has two swords."

The man shook his head. "Haven't seen anyone like that."

Even though they had a lead, no news of her friends left Suzanne disappointed. She hadn't realized how worried she was about the two of them. While she was a prisoner in Fenhold, her own safety had been a priority. And then she had been overwhelmed by the gray. But now that she had time to think, she had time to worry for her friends.

Still, if they could find Burgrave, then maybe she could log them out without having to find them at all. Maybe she should stick with Crux so she could get the key to the Oracle Chamber.

The family came out from behind the table and took seats around the table. Suzanne sat with them, but Crux was far too large to fit.

"Thanks for your help," Suzanne said. "Sorry about coming in like we did, but it didn't look like anyone was going to speak with us."

"Well, he did say that anyone asking about him would be working for Ramses," the woman shrugged. "And we don't want much to do with the king. But if you lot work for Ramses then I can't see us able to say no. You'd probably just feed us to your big friend there."

"Oh no!" Crux said, looking mortified. "I would never eat you!"

"That's good," the kid said. A deep understanding seemed to pass between him and Crux.

As reluctant as she was to ruin the moment, Suzanne felt that finding Burgrave should take precedence. "Where was this guy going?" she asked.

"West," the woman answered. "Right to the river. He suggested we follow him. Said something about getting away from King Ramses."

Well, you won't have to worry about that, Suzanne thought. None of the Altairi would have to worry about Ramses ever again.

But how could they be sure it was Burgrave who had passed by? The last thing they wanted to do was follow some random short NPC all the way across Io just to discover it wasn't the right one. They had to be sure. And one feature of Burgrave's stuck out to Suzanne more than all the others.

"This NPC," Suzanne said. "Do you remember what his eyes were like?"

"Of course," the man answered. "All gray. Never seen anyone else like that."

"That's him," she said, exhaling in relief. "Listen, you need to leave this village as soon as possible. Go as far north as you can. Something terrible is coming."

"What?" the woman asked, her eyes wide with fear. "What is it?"

Suzanne didn't know how to begin explaining the graying to the NPCs. "Just believe me. Tell everyone you can to leave. You've got to get out of here while you still can."

Shortly after, they left the village, following the road west again.

"So, we're going to have to fight this monster," Suzanne explained. "He's tough but we should be able to take him. He's called the Lord of Lily Pads, and when we beat him it will make a bridge to Pyxis."

At least she hoped it would. Suzanne didn't know how they would get across if that part of the game was glitching too.

"You know a lot for someone from far away," Crux said.

Suzanne was used to NPCs being surprised by her knowledge. She always gave vague answers when pressed for information, but with Crux, she didn't think she had much to worry about. He was simply making an observation and soon became preoccupied again with fallen leaves.

As the land sloped down to the river, Suzanne felt herself growing strangely excited for the upcoming fight. Like all the boss monsters, she designed the Lord of Lily Pads personally. She knew everything the frog monster could do and was looking forward to seeing how her design turned out.

But when they reached the shore of the Ion River, the Lord of Lily Pads was nowhere to be seen. He was supposed to appear to high-level player characters if they were this far south on the river, but after ten minutes Suzanne had to admit he just wasn't going to show.

Crux expressed her impatience for her. "How long must we wait?" he lamented. "I want to see Pyxis and hit monsters."

Suzanne didn't have an answer for him. She walked up to the Ion River's edge and ran her fingers through the water. As she did, the water began to roil.

Finally, she thought. But instead of a large frog, a series of lily pads rose up from the depths, forming a bridge across.

"I thought we had to kill the Lily Pad King?" Crux asked. "The bridge is already here."

Suzanne was nearly as shocked as he was. The Lord of Lily Pads would only appear to player characters, and then only that character and others in their party could use the bridge. But if the bridge was appearing for Suzanne, that meant someone in her party had taken the boss out.

It must have been Brit and Mikayla! They were okay. And more than that, they had to be in Pyxis! She explained her theory to Crux, who seemed to understand. At least he understood to follow her when she set off across the lily pads to the Pyxian shore.

If Brit and Mikayla had come this way, that probably meant they were going to New Pyxia. But they also could have been going to Vale. Suzanne didn't know whether to go due west or northwest toward the Pyxian mountains. The best move would be to angle between the Capital and the mountains, so she could check the nearby towns for news of her friends.

Crux had another idea. "Glensia is a little south of here. We should go that way," he said, pointing southwest, away from everywhere Suzanne wanted to go.

"No," she said. "Burgrave can wait. Let's find Brit and Mikayla first."

Crux shook his head. "You promised we would find Burgrave. I want to find Burgrave. You said would help me and now you have to help me."

Suzanne didn't know how she could argue with Crux. If they didn't move quickly, they might lose Brit and Mikayla's trail. But once she had the key to the Oracle Chamber that wouldn't matter. The notion of rescuing the two of them, without them ever knowing, was particularly tempting to her.

But, really, what convinced her was the fact that she needed the key. Suzanne couldn't remember the hours she had spent in the throne room in Zenith City, trying everything she could to unlock the Oracle Chamber. Burgrave had the key. If she let him get away now, she might never get another shot at finding him, especially if Burgrave didn't want to be found. And Glensia wasn't that far from New Pyxia. If it turned out be a dead end she could always head north and ask Leo and Lynx for their help.

"Okay," she said, "but we're going to have to travel fast. We don't want to miss Burgrave."

The look of joy on Crux's face did a little to alleviate Suzanne's guilty conscience. *We'll be back together soon*, she promised Brit and Mikayla, she promised herself. And then they could all go home.

Chapter 10

"Britney?"

Fuck, Brit thought. *Gimme another ten minutes. At least.*

Without opening her eyes, Brit reached behind her for one of the throw pillows littering her bed. She buried her head in chintz, muting all sound. She was at constant war with these pillows. Every night she threw them on the floor, but each afternoon, upon returning from school, they were back, arranged in their neat little rows. Some days she could have sworn they had procreated in her absence.

Thoughts of their destruction often tempted

Brit. She fantasized about chopping the pillows up, throwing them in a blender, setting the blender to fricassee and watching in glee as the whirling blades ripped the pillows to shreds. Who needed so many pillows anyway?

"Britney?"

Her mother's voice was louder this time. Brit sighed through the pillow and let it fall from her hands. Her mother wasn't going to go away.

"Don't make me call you a third time!"

The tone was chipper, even saccharine, but Brit could detect the edge in her mother's voice. Her mom had shouted her name so many times that Brit knew all its variations. Sweet, like this wasn't the shit hitting the fan, but Brit had at most five minutes to appear or the situation would go nuclear.

And as much as Brit wanted her sleep, she dreaded the fight more. *Fight* was the wrong word. It implied that what followed would be a two-sided affair, which wasn't the case. Her mother called the shouting matches "our little spats" in polite company, but Brit thought that was even stupider than calling them a *fight*. To Brit, they would always be bitch fits.

The bitching wouldn't last long. Brit had school in thirty minutes and her mother would never let her be late for that. Reluctantly, clinging to the last minute of darkness, Brit opened her eyes.

She was already dressed. But not in her clothes. She was wearing a neat tartan skirt and a white blouse with an immaculately pressed collar. The cherry on top of this shit sundae was the matching sweater vest, emblazoned with the coat of arms of The Meadowbridge Academy for Young Women.

Brit was used to the passive-aggressive gestures of her mother, but this was taking things way too far. Brit hadn't seen, let alone worn, her Meadowbridge uniform since they kicked her out. Not that she was sorry to go—quite the opposite, she was laughing as security escorted her out of the building—but she thought she had thrown out her private school duds long ago.

Well, this is going to be fun, Brit thought. If her mom thought she was going to stand for this bullshit then she must have had an aneurysm. Brit swung her feet to the floor and stood up, before realizing that this wasn't her room anymore.

Half of it was. Her bed was still her bed. Her dresser was in the same corner as always, half her clothes sticking out of it. Opposite the dresser was her desk, or the mound of clothes and crap that covered her desk at least. Her posters were all up in their usual places too.

But she was pretty sure her floor was carpeted, not stone. She was certain her walls were painted and not stone either. And Brit knew, for a fact, that the door to her room was a door and not the crossbars of a jail cell.

The cell door swung open. Brit backed up, stumbling and falling back into the bed. On cue, the sheets wrapped themselves around her arms and legs. A horde of kobolds poured into the room, hissing and spitting, their scimitars drawn. *These are the biggest kobolds I've ever seen,* Brit thought, struggling to free herself from the tangled sheets. The more she struggled, the tighter she was caught.

The biggest of the lizard-men opened its mouth, but in place of its normal reptilian cry, it called her name. "Britney?" Its voice sounded exactly like her mother.

Brit shuddered and struggled against her restraints. The kobolds advanced. "Britney?" the big one called again. Now it was harsher, crueler, mocking. She saw his scimitar raise and winced. Her arms came free of the sheet and Brit threw them in front of her for protection.

She heard the clank of metal on metal and opened her eyes again—somehow she was now wearing her armor and the blade had glanced off a gauntlet.

"My turn!" She vaulted her feet into the kobold's chest, sending it sprawling. She sprang back up and slammed a fist into the next kobold. Her punch hit it in the knee.

But how was that possible? Craning her neck back she saw that the kobold now towered over her, easily the height of a building. The roof of the room zoomed away from her at a dizzying pace.

The kobold raised its foot. The shadow swept over her. There was nowhere to run.

Brit opened her eyes.

She remembered. There were no throw pillows, no kobolds. Her mother's voice echoed in her ears, or was it the kobold's voice? The echo faded and with it she was fully awake, the last remnant of her dream gone. She wasn't in her bed, her room, her world. She was in the guest quarters of Leo's castle, in New Pyxia, in Io.

Brit rolled out of bed, reconnecting with her character's body. She had dreamt she was back to her actual size and it took her a moment to reac-quaint herself with being a Dragoon. Castle Pyxia's curtain walls swayed slowly in unison, expanding and deflating like a pair of lungs. She waited for her eyes to adjust to the darkness before standing up.

Mikayla slept in the other bed. As Brit's eyes adjusted to the dark, she could see that Mikayla was still asleep. Somehow Brit found that reas-suring just to see her there. So few things were playing out as she expected lately. Brit was glad she had Mikayla to rely on.

Three days. Three days in the court of King Leo and all they had gotten him to do was promise he would help Suzanne, "As soon as I am able." Brit smelled bullshit. He was the king of Pyxis after all. All he had to do was make the decision and his army would march. But every day, Xenos had another reason to delay action.

Leo always listened. It was enough to drive Brit mad. She wasn't going to be able to hold her temper back much longer. Mikayla knew it was happening—she had suggested Brit sit this latest meeting out, not wanting her to snap Xenos in two. Brit had taken to the streets of New Pyxia to try and find out more information, but all the Citizens fed her the same bland lines about how happy they were to see her. She could have gotten more useful info talking to a kobold.

Brit sighed. In the morning, she was going to have a talk with Mikayla about their next move. They couldn't just sit here twiddling their thumbs, waiting for Leo to come to his senses. Suzanne was counting on them.

She knew she wouldn't be getting back to sleep. With one last look at Mikayla, she pushed the curtains apart and stepped out of their room. In the hallway, Brit equipped her armor. She doubted she needed it—Xenos hadn't tried anything, and Leo's guards patrolled the castle regularly. But Brit always felt naked in Io without her armor on.

Brit felt her way down the staircase, through

the maze of curtains on the ground floor and out of the castle's main entrance. She'd been in Castle Pyxia long enough that the guards she ran into let her pass without comment.

Out in the night air, she felt calmer. Small waves rolled over the moat. On the other side of the water she saw the torchlit streets and canals of New Pyxia. But the drawbridge was up, and there were no NPCs in sight to ferry her across. Besides, Brit didn't want to leave Mikayla alone in the castle. Yet there was somewhere else she could go.

With one hand on the castle to steady herself in the darkness, Brit walked around the perimeter of the island. Halfway around she came into a secluded garden illuminated by the full moon.

Pale light washed the colors of the flowerbeds, softening the sharp reds and blues of the buds. The moonlight was also caught in the water of a fountain, glittering like the stars in the cloudless sky. The night was as still as it was clear; she could hear the faint splashing of an oarsman paddling through the city and distant voices calling out to each other on the darkened streets. She walked over to the flowers and plucked one, holding it up to her nose and inhaling. She couldn't smell anything. Suzanne probably hadn't gotten that far in programming the game before they were trapped. Brit thought it was funny how she had gotten used to random monsters and fighting with a halberd, but the lack of smell still surprised her.

How much longer can we sit around on our asses? Every day they spent in Pyxis was another day they left her in captivity. *Tomorrow, we'll leave,* she told herself. *Even if it's just the two of us, we have to try. Leo's not going to help us.*

The flower petals fell from Brit's hand. She looked down. Without realizing it, she had crushed the flower. As the last petals fluttered to the ground, they distorted, stretching until they snapped into clouds of pixels. The pixels floated up, vanishing in front of Brit's eyes.

Is that what's going to happen to us? Since they got trapped in Io, there had been some close calls, but the girls were still all relatively fine. Well, Brit was assuming Suzanne was fine. But if Suzanne really was hurt, Brit thought she would know. She couldn't explain it, just like how she couldn't explain her dreams, but somehow she knew it was true. If Suzanne had died already, then Brit would have known.

Brit heard the bushes rustling in the breeze. She almost ignored it, but the night was still. None of the flowers were bending with a breeze and Brit definitely couldn't feel one on her face. Someone else was in the garden. Trying to make her movements look casual, Brit backed herself up against the domed wall of Pyxia Castle.

She could feel her heart beating faster in her chest. She wasn't afraid, she was excited. Brit couldn't help the grin growing on her face. So much of Io was crazy and out of her control; it was almost a relief to take her health bar into her own hands. Fighting was when Io felt the most like a game to her.

But now wasn't the time to lose her focus. She saw a shadow dart between two trees. The figure stepped into the moonlight for a second, long enough for Brit to see the grey icon spinning over its head, marking it as an NPC. Brit kept her eyes on the trees while she opened up her inventory and grabbed her halberd out of it. The halberd stood as tall as Brit herself, with a razor-sharp axe blade and a thick spitting spike.

Three flashes flew out of the shadows. Brit threw herself to the side as the throwing knives embedded themselves in the stone where she had been standing. Brit sprang back up to standing as the NPC launched itself at her from the trees. It passed in front of the moon. Brit swung her halberd at the silhouette and felt the vibrations from a clean hit travel down the pole to her arms.

"You're faster than you look," the NPC said, her voice cold with disdain.

Brit knew that voice. "I figured you'd be lurking somewhere nearby Xenos. What are you two really doing here, Gemini?" she demanded of the masked Assassin. Gemini was another servant of the Altairi king, Ramses, an Assassin who never showed her face.

"I could ask you the same thing," Gemini said as she stood up and brushed the dirt from her cloak. Even standing in the moonlight, the Assassin's long black cloak made it hard for Brit to size her up. "Isn't Suzanne still in Altair?" Gemini taunted. "And here you and Mikayla are, on the other side of the world. Aren't you worried about your friend?"

Brit didn't think: she moved. She charged at Gemini, raising her halberd high. But although Brit was twice her size, she was nowhere near as fast as the Assassin. Her hacking swing sliced nothing but air. Gemini ducked low and slashed at Brit's ankles, toppling her to the ground.

Brit flailed out with her feet, kicking at Gemini.

Nothing connected but it gave her the space she needed to get back up. By the time she was standing again, Gemini had melted back into the shadows.

"This is going to be fun," the Assassin cackled. Brit couldn't tell where Gemini's voice was coming from. Standing in the middle of the garden, she could be attacked from any side. She had to get her back up against something.

Brit took a cautious step toward the dome of Pyxia Castle, heard rustling and froze in place. The rustling stopped. Brit tried to stifle her growing frustration. If Gemini would just fight her in the open . . . but then, she knew exactly why the Assassin wouldn't do that. *But if I can make her come out from behind cover . . .* Brit knew exactly what she had to do.

Brit took another step toward the castle, then another. She knew she would have to pass under the trees to get there. If Gemini was hiding in one of them it would give the Assassin an easy opportunity to drop down and attack her. Just as she suspected, when Brit stepped under the branches of the first tree, she heard the rustling sound again.

She looked up to see Gemini falling through the canopy, cloak thrown back to reveal her two curved daggers. Brit dropped her halberd and grabbed for the Assassin's waist. She felt pain lance through her shoulders as the Assassin's blades sunk in, but she didn't let go. Brit let herself fall backwards, her back slamming into the ground. She rolled over and pinned Gemini to the ground beneath her.

Gemini tried to jerk her arms loose; she kicked with all her might, but Brit knew the Assassin wouldn't be able to get free.

"We're going to have a little chat," Brit said.

"Like I would tell you anything."

Brit let go of Gemini's left arm and punched the Assassin in the face. She must not have known her own strength because the Assassin's mask cracked in two. It distorted and pixilated, leaving nothing but a cloud of pixels behind.

What Brit saw made her freeze, giving Gemini

enough time to wriggle out of Brit's grasp. The Assassin backed away from Brit, drawing two more daggers out of her belt.

"Don't tell me," Gemini said, "I'm gorgeous."

Brit said nothing, it was all too dumbfounding. Staring back at her, with hatred etched into every line of her face, was Suzanne. But it wasn't quite Suzanne. Her voice sounded different, and she was an Assassin, not an Infiltrator, and a red icon twirled over her head instead of a green one. Still, the NPC in front of Brit looked more like the real world Suzanne than even Suzanne's character did.

"You can't be . . . " Brit's voice trailed off, she had no other words.

"Can't be what?" Suzanne's face sneered.

Brit shook her head, trying to concentrate. "If I knew my face would shut you down, I would have ditched the mask a long time ago," Gemini laughed.

Brit heard footsteps coming from within the castle. Their fight must have alerted the castle guard. Sure enough, NPCs streamed out of Pyxia Castle. They wore long, flowing Pyxian robes. Most were in the Ranger classes, armed with small round shields and curved swords.

"Listen," Brit called to the NPCs. "This is Gemini. She's works for Ramses! You can't let her get away."

None of the NPCs moved. It was like they hadn't heard.

Brit's stomach sank as she heard more of Gemini's soft laughter and saw another NPC step out of the castle. His hood was pulled low over his face.

"The Dragoon is an enemy of Pyxis," Xenos said. "She is most dangerous. Take care while apprehending her."

Brit realized her halberd was back by the trees where she had dropped it. She knocked the nearest Pyxian off his feet with a punch, but another grabbed on to her arm. Brit fought desperately, throwing one off her back to the ground, but it was a lost cause. The Pyxians swarmed her, pinning her to the ground as she had pinned Gemini only minutes earlier. They wrenched her arms behind her back, tying them with thick rope. She was pulled roughly up to her knees.

"Take care of Mikayla," she heard Xenos say to Gemini, as the Pyxians put a sack over her head and returned her to darkness. Brit bucked, trying to throw the NPCs off of her. Yet there were too many, and she heard the footsteps of still more, coming to hold her down.

"She's devil strong," she heard an NPC say, laughing. Brit lashed out with her foot and felt savage satisfaction as the NPC yelped in pain.

Xenos said, "Quiet her." Stars erupted in the darkness as the butt end of a spear smashed into Brit's face. She nearly fell over but managed to stay on her knees.

"Fuck you," she spat. She got another blow to the head in reply.

"Careful!" Xenos said. "Do not kill her until I have spoken to the king."

The next thing Brit knew, she was being carried none too gently by the NPCs. She could tell they were going downstairs, jostled by each step. The air was growing colder. She could see nothing through her hood. Flexing her muscles, she realized her legs were now tied together as well. Brit's chest grew tight with panic. Where were they taking her? She squirmed, trying to free herself from their grasps.

"This one won't quit!" one of the NPCs complained.

"She wriggles anymore and I say we let her fall the rest of the way down," another replied.

Brit didn't stop fighting; her legs swung out and kicked what felt like a face. More cursing followed and she fell heavily, her hip banging into a cold stone step.

She lay dazed, waiting for them to grab her. But no hand touched her. Then she heard the Pyxians shouting in confusion and a sound like whistling.

Brit waited. Whatever was happening to the NPCs would happen to her soon enough. The fighting above ended and she heard soft footsteps descending toward her.

Torchlight blinded Brit as the sack was pulled off her head. Blinking through the glare she saw her savior: a blond NPC, her hair done up in a bun. Slung over her shoulders was a double-bladed pole weapon Brit had only ever seen one NPC use.

"Lynx," Brit said.

Lynx smiled. Her smile looked an awful lot like her brother Leo's.

"You have no idea how happy I am to see you," Lynx said.

Chapter 11

It had been more than an hour and Brit still hadn't returned. Mikayla wasn't surprised. This wasn't the first time Brit had wandered off; Mikayla couldn't keep track of the number of times she woke up in the middle of the night and Brit wasn't there. But Brit would always return before dawn. Judging by the first lights that were just slipping in through the high windows of Castle Pyxia, dawn wouldn't be much longer in coming. Mikayla could wait until then.

One day she would confront Brit about what she did at night. That would be when she'd mention the other thing, that she heard Brit talking in her sleep. Mikayla remembered sleepovers with Brit from the real world. Brit was a snorer, not a talker. Most nights in Io, Brit mumbled words, but sometimes whole sentences slipped out.

Mikayla first noticed the change while traveling through the wilderness of Io, taking turns keeping watch at night. As far as Mikayla knew, when she went to sleep that was it, lights out. Her character's body shut down until she woke up herself or was woken. Brit was a dynamic sleeper, tossing and turning, muttering to herself, almost as if she was dreaming. But Mikayla remembered Suzanne saying something about them not being able to dream in-game. Her own nights in Io had all been dreamless. Well, whatever. Mikayla leaned back into her pillow, resolving to ask Brit about it all in the morning.

She watched the curtain walls, letting their rhythmic swaying lull her to unconsciousness . . . then she saw the shadow. The silhouette was perched at the intersection of two curtain walls, balanced on the rope that the curtains hung from. It was a cloudless night, like all the others in Pyxis. Either a bird was flying in place between the moon and the window, or someone was hiding in the corner, using an Energite move to keep the light off of themselves.

As much as she hoped otherwise, Mikayla bet it was the latter. She propped herself up on her elbows to make sure she wouldn't inadvertently put her character to sleep. A voice inside told her she was just being paranoid, but her experience in Io taught that you could never be too careful. It had to be an NPC: the shadow remained perfectly still. Even with her heightened vision it remained obscure.

Mikayla heard a soft snap—the sound of a blade leaving its sheath—and threw herself out of bed. Three knives sprouted from the headboard, where her torso had just been. A second slower . . . no, she couldn't afford to think like that. Now it was time to fight.

The shadow had already dropped from its perch to the floor and was approaching her slowly. Mikayla reached into her inventory and drew her sword. She jabbed at her assailant's head, but the NPC ducked under the blade.

She's fast, Mikayla thought, springing backwards out of range. She felt the curtain wall at her back, no support at all. She barely had time to get her other sword before the NPC lunged at her with a curved knife. Mikayla parried the slash, but the NPC landed a kick on her ribs, knocking the wind out of her.

Mikayla saw her health bar dip. *That was just a kick*, she thought. *How did it do so much damage?* The NPC turned, ready to strike again, but this time Mikayla was prepared. She leapt to the side as the NPC charged and slashed the curtain, sending it tumbling down on her assailant. She heard the NPC shout in rage as she cut the sides free, entangling the NPC. Moonlight streamed through the hole in the wall, making an easy target.

Mikayla stabbed. She felt the usual twinge of satisfaction and regret that came when the point of her sword found its way into an NPC's body.

But whoever she was fighting wouldn't go down that easily. She stabbed again; the NPC threw herself sideways and rolled away, disentangling herself in the process. With the full light of the moon, Mikayla could see her opponent was a member of the Rogue classes, which explained her speed and weapon choice. But then the NPC looked up, dropping the shredded remains of the curtain to the floor. Mikayla couldn't believe what she was seeing: Suzanne's face stared at her.

It was Suzanne's face and it wasn't. The features—the small nose, big brown eyes, and thin lips—were all Suzanne's. Not Suzanne's character in Io, but Suzanne Thurston's from the real world. But the expression was something Mikayla had never seen in any reality. The NPC with Suzanne's face stared at her with absolute loathing, the eyes narrowed in disdain, the mouth curled up into a sneer of hatred.

Mikayla didn't have time to figure it all out. She barely had time to raise her sword and block the NPC's next attack, a downward slice. The NPC attacked again and again and it was all Mikayla could do to dodge the big strikes. She saw her health falling to chip damage and cursed herself for being too passive. She wouldn't get through this fight just trying not to lose. Her opponent fought with knives, which gave her the advantage up close. Mikayla had to get the initiative back somehow, which meant moving the fight to somewhere with more room to maneuver.

Mikayla feinted a lunge. The NPC knocked her blade aside and stepped in for a counter-attack, but Mikayla followed her momentum and kept running, through the hole in the curtain and out into the hallway.

She ran for the stairs. She had to find Brit—her nighttime stroll seemed less idyllic now. Mikayla reached the top of the landing and started down the steps when she heard stampeding feet running up toward her.

A whole squadron of guards came into view—Pyxians. They stared up at her like she was a stranger and hadn't spent the last week as a guest of their king. At the front of the group was Elias the Swiftblade.

"Help!" she called to him. "Someone is attacking me!"

Elias drew his sword. He stepped forward and leveled the blade at her. "You are under arrest for drawing steel in the court of King Leo. Throw down your weapons and come peacefully."

"What?" She heard a quiet shuffle of feet and looked back for the Assassin, but she was gone. How had she vanished like that? Mikayla saw that the damage from their fight had spilled out into the hallway. She could hear sounds of stirring; they had woken up other NPCs. It looked like she had some explaining to do.

"What are you looking at?" Elias demanded. "Throw down your swords. You—"

"Are under arrest," Mikayla finished for him. "Yeah, yeah, I know." She couldn't see the Assassin anywhere. She might as well go with the guards. At least with Leo she would have a chance to explain herself. She sheathed her swords and walked toward Elias.

The Swiftblade turned to an NPC at the back of the formation. "Go tell Xenos we have apprehended Mikayla."

They aren't working for Leo, they're working for Xenos! It occurred to her that those two things might be the same, but she had to hope that they weren't. Her hand drifted back toward the hilt of her sword.

"Do not think about it," Elias snapped. There was none of his earlier obsequiousness in his tone. "If you do not come peacefully we will be required to use force."

"Just try it," Mikayla said.

Elias snarled and threw himself at her. Her first sword checked his strike, turning it aside. With her other blade she slashed at his throat. He fell to his knees. Mikayla kicked him backwards onto his men. They stumbled over their leader, giving her time to run back the way she came.

NPCs were now coming out of their rooms. A matronly NPC, brandishing a battle axe, stepped out into the hallway. Mikayla didn't give her a chance to swing it, running past full-tilt. She knew there was only one way down from this floor and that was the stairs. That meant the only direction she had to go was up.

Mikayla ran three steps up the wall, jumping off and grabbing for the rope from which the curtains hung. Pulling herself up, she ran down the rope. She jumped, landing and stretching the rope out, which launched her high enough to grab for one of the windows. Head first, she climbed out onto the roof of Castle Pyxia.

Now what? Mikayla wondered.

As if on cue, a dagger flew at her. She blocked it with the hilt of her sword, trying not to imagine the distance it fell from the roof to the ground.

"The next thing off the roof will be you." The Assassin was standing at the top of the dome, her daggers gleaming with moonlight, the sneer on her face settled into a mocking grin. In a flash, Mikayla knew who she was.

"Hey, Gemini," Mikayla said. She took a step up the slope of the roof, carefully. The last thing she wanted was to lose her footing.

"Just hey? No witty comeback? I guess that's more Brit's speed. Still, I'm disappointed in you, Mikayla. Why didn't you just cut through those Pyxians? We both know you could have handled them."

The longer Mikayla stared at her, the easier it was to distinguish the NPC from Suzanne's game character. Also, hearing Gemini speak really reinforced the difference.

"Maybe I'm not a psycho like you," Mikayla said. She was halfway up the dome.

"No one's like me," Gemini said, launching herself at Mikayla. Their blades met. For a moment, Gemini had her entire bodyweight behind her blades, but Mikayla held strong and pushed back. The Assassin sprung off and landed gracefully on her feet further down the dome.

"You could have fooled me," Mikayla said. "With a face like that. What's up with that, anyway? Trying to seduce Leo or something?"

Gemini sprang at her again, slashing with such savagery that Mikayla had to take a step back. "You think I wanted to look like this?" she demanded. "You think I had a choice?"

She sliced at Mikayla's waist. Mikayla flipped her sword around to block, then punched Gemini in the nose with its hilt. The Assassin staggered backwards, clutching her face.

"I don't really give a shit," Mikayla said. "Tell me where Brit is and I won't throw you off the roof."

"She wasn't in such good shape when I was

done with her. I expect Xenos has gotten what he wants out of her by now," Gemini sneered. "Try checking the canals."

Part of Mikayla knew Gemini was just trying to goad her, but most of Mikayla didn't care. Both of them lashed out with their blades, steel clashing against steel. Feint and lunge, parry, rolling dives to the side: it was like they were engaged in an intricate dance.

Mikayla's eyes flitted to her health bar and she saw it over halfway gone. *Don't be stupid*, she told herself. *You can't take many more hits.*

"Ready to give up?" Gemini shouted. Despite her bravado, Mikayla could see the Assassin breathing hard. She had taken a fair amount of damage as well. Mikayla didn't have an encyclo-pedic knowledge of the classes like Suzanne did, but she knew that anything Rogue-related wasn't designed to take tons of damage.

Mikayla had never been up on the roof before. New Pyxia was beautiful from this angle, the moonlit canals like silver veins, pumped through the city's heart. She wondered if this is what Leo saw when he came up here, if he came up here. Below, she could see two figures running out of Castle Pyxia toward the docks. She heard the echo of her name shouted from below.

A crazy idea sprang into her head. Something she would never do. Something that Brit would do in a heartbeat.

Well, Mikayla thought, *I hope this works.*

They charged at each other again. Mikayla stabbed at Gemini's feet. The Assassin leaped back, but Mikayla charged forward, wrapping her arms around Gemini's waist, tackling. She felt a dagger go into her back but ignored the pain, ignored her health dropping.

"What are you doing?" Gemini shouted. "You're going to kill us!"

Mikayla didn't answer. She threw her whole weight off the roof, dragging Gemini down with her. For a moment, they fell together, but then the Assassin kicked off her and fell away into darkness. Mikayla saw the ground rushing up toward her and heard her best friend's voice shouting her name.

"Mikayla!"

The wind was knocked out of her as she landed, not on the ground, but in two massive, gentle arms.

"I've got you!" Brit shouted. "I've got you."

Mikayla's head was swimming. "Where's Gemini?" she asked weakly.

"I don't know," Brit said, carrying her away from the dome. "Are you okay?"

Mikayla glanced around. Almost all of her health bar was gone, and apparently so was the Assassin. The moon bounced off of Brit's hair, casting it in silver light.

"You look really pretty," Mikayla said.

She felt Brit's arms stiffen beneath her. Brit stopped in her tracks.

"We need to be gone, like yesterday," Brit said.

"The boat is up ahead," another voice said.

"Who's that?" Mikayla asked. Her eyes weren't working so well anymore.

"Lynx is here," Brit said. "Stay calm. I've got a health potion somewhere. You're going to be fine."

"I know," Mikayla said. "I'm with you."

She wrapped her arms around Brit's neck and pulled herself up, so they were face to face.

"What are you . . . ?" Brit muttered, her eyes flitting between Mikayla and the path.

"Thanks for catching me," Mikayla said. She kissed her. She felt Brit stop running, shocked, and then the potion kicked in and she passed out.

Chapter 12

Brit was having a hard time focusing on what the Pyxians were saying. She kept stealing looks at Mikayla. They were seated around a tree stump, serving as a makeshift table and map, while Lynx sketched out her plan with a whittling knife. Mikayla was seated opposite Brit, with Mallon to her left, and Rigel to her right. Brit sat between Alphonse and Lynx, but she might as well have been on the moon for how much she followed what they were saying.

It was strange finding herself among so many old allies again. She hadn't seen Alphonse or Mallon since the last days of the war between Pyxis and

Altair. Yet when Lynx lead them through a secret passage out of New Pyxia, Alphonse was waiting for them. They spared no time with pleasantries, traveling hard for a day to the pre-scouted safe area. There they met up with Rigel and Mallon to discuss their plans.

What those plans were, though, Brit couldn't say. Mikayla appeared engrossed in the princess's words, but she was a pro at pretending to pay attention. How many times had Brit seen her fake it through boring classes at Perry Hall High with nothing but a bland look of engagement and a smile when called on?

She has to be thinking about it, Brit told herself. *She has to.*

Mikayla turned and looked at her and smiled. Brit felt a fluttering in her chest.

"Brit?" Mikayla said. "How does that sound?"

Oh crap. Brit realized the Pyxians were all staring at her expectantly, waiting for her to answer. She racked her mind for some bullshit. A smile crept across Mikayla's face, not unkind, but pointed all the same.

"Why don't you run through it one more time," Mikayla said to Lynx. "I'm not sure I got all of it."

Brit nodded, still finding it difficult to put two words together.

"Very well," Lynx said. "We head east to the Pyxian camp. The Pyxians have more cause than most to disdain my brother's rule. You, Brit, and I will gather allies from among them. Meanwhile, Rigel will return to Vale. He will try to sway the garrison there against Leo. If he succeeds, then we will be able to attack New Pyxia from the north and south simultaneously, closing it off from any reinforcements Xenos might summon."

"But what about Suzanne?" Brit asked.

Lynx made a little frown. "Perhaps after we take New Pyxia we can turn our attention to Altair."

Suzanne can't wait that long, Brit thought. The look on Mikayla's face showed she agreed. But before she could voice her disapproval, Alphonse, a burly NPC who had fought with them at The Floating Eye, banged his axe on the stump.

"It is too dangerous for you to travel alone," he said to Lynx. "If Xenos's forces discover you, then they will kill you, and all will be lost."

"I will not be alone," Lynx replied. "Brit and Mikayla will accompany me."

Alphonse snorted derisively.

What the fuck? Brit thought. She wasn't best friends with the Pyxian, but they had always been on the same side. Alphonse was a fierce fighter and she respected that. What was his issue?

"You are sure you can trust them?"

"Of course she can trust us," Brit cut in. "But Lynx, we can't just forget about Suzanne. She's Ramses's prisoner! Who knows how long he's going to keep her around!"

"She is no prisoner," Alphonse replied.

"Excuse me?" Mikayla said. "I'm pretty sure she is."

"And I am confident she is not," he spat back.

Mallon, an older NPC who handled reconnaissance for the Pyxians during the war, cleared her throat. "We have received reports of Suzanne operating in Pyxis. She was seen south of the Capital, near a town called Glensia."

Brit found Mikayla's eyes and saw confusion in them matching her own. Why would Ramses move Suzanne to Pyxis? But then it clicked into place.

"It wasn't Suzanne!" Brit said. "It was Gemini!"

She explained what she had seen the night they escaped New Pyxia, how the Assassin was nearly identical to Suzanne. Mikayla backed her up, but even still, the Pyxians didn't seem convinced.

"Even if what you saw is true," Alphonse said, "that proves nothing! Suzanne was reported miles away from the Capital! How could she be in two places at once?"

Brit crossed her arms. "When we left Fenhold, Xenos was there, but Leo had said Xenos hadn't left New Pyxia when we showed up. You want to explain that?"

"Perhaps this Gemini can also wear Xenos's face!" Alphonse roared back.

"Enough," Lynx said. Brit thought she heard something of Libra in Lynx's tone. "Brit, Mikayla, there is another possibility. Suzanne could have turned. I do not know how Xenos does it, but he changes us. Who would know better than me? My brother was never a tyrant, and yet here we are, plotting his downfall. I hope you are right and Suzanne is still a prisoner. But we cannot prioritize rescuing someone who might be fighting against us. First, we must save our home."

But it isn't our home, Brit thought bitterly.

"What if we compromise?" Mikayla suggested. She had been studying the map. "Glensia is maybe a day's journey out of the way. If we don't find anything in Glensia, we'll all head east to the Pyxian camp."

Lynx nodded her approval, but Alphonse still glowered.

"Then I am going with you," Alphonse growled. "I will not leave you unguarded, Lynx."

"You would leave Rigel to travel alone?"

"Begging your pardon, Princess," Rigel said. "But I think I can manage on my own. After all, the lot of you are wanted criminals. But me, I am just an old smith watching over a mountain for his king. As far as Leo knows I am still his man."

"Then I might as well go east," Mallon said. "After all, King Leo cannot be too pleased with me either. I would not want to spoil your cover, Rigel."

This earned a laugh from the other Pyxians.

"Someone want to fill us in on the joke?" Brit asked.

"After I first disappeared from the Capital," Lynx explained, "my brother set Mallon on finding me. She continuously fed him the wrong information. He wasted weeks sending soldiers to the far corners of our land, all to come back empty-handed."

"When Leo found out I imagine he was a little

upset," Mallon chuckled. "But by then I had split off myself, so who could he send to find me?"

Brit noticed Alphonse alone wasn't laughing. "He grasps blindly but that does not lessen his fist," Alphonse said. "He checks up on every rumor of you. Those he suspects of hiding you suffer."

His words sobered the Pyxians. "All the more reason not to waste time," Lynx said. "We must go now, and quickly."

By then night was falling again. Brit was ready to hit the road, but she could see the Pyxians were all fading.

Rigel appeared to be of the same opinion. "We ought to rest now while we still have the chance," he said.

While they set up tents, Brit volunteered for the first watch. She wasn't tired and wanted some time alone to think. The NPCs disappeared with a quick goodnight and fell asleep immediately.

Brit sat with her back to a tree, the fire crackling low before her. Tomorrow they'd be traveling again, and hard. It was stupid, really. They'd gone to Pyxis to find help and all they had done was turn their biggest ally against them. She could feel herself getting entangled in another war, another fight that wasn't her own.

But what was her fight? She gazed over at the tent where Mikayla was sleeping. They were fighting to get home, back to reality. And Brit wasn't so sure she wanted to rush that return. Once they were back in the real world, she would be a high school student again. Sleepwalking through classes, fighting with her mom, and blowing off homework to game. She wouldn't be looking for an escape from danger but from the opposite.

And what about Mikayla?

Brit would be lying if she said she hadn't felt this way for a while. Whenever Mikayla developed a crush on a new guy, Brit had always felt a weird desire to kick him in the nuts. Sure, that was mostly because they were neanderthals. But as she sat alone in the Pyxian wilderness, Brit had to wonder if she'd always known there was some jealousy mixed in there.

She's your best friend, she told herself. *You really want to risk ruining that?*

But it could be different, another voice argued. *Things might change.*

But things never did. Even in Io, things never changed. They were fighting another war, going on another quest, trying to reach the next level, trying to stay alive. But at least in Io, she wasn't stuck in the suburbs, stuck in classrooms. She wasn't stuck watching the world drag Mikayla away: away to cheerleading practices, away to some fancy college, away from Brit.

We're just stuck in Io. She laughed softly.

"What's so funny?"

Brit started kicking leaves and twigs into the fire. The flames flared, spitting and snapping. Mikayla dropped down from the tree and sat cross-legged by the flames.

"If I was Gemini you'd be dead by now," she said.

Brit shook her head. "If you were Gemini you'd have given yourself away gloating, just the same."

Mikayla smiled thinly. "I'm only half-joking. You're on watch, you should be more careful."

Brit shrugged as Mikayla sat down near her. All Brit had to do was lean over to touch her. "Well, shouldn't you be sleeping?"

"I wasn't tired," Mikayla said. "Well, no. I guess I am. I didn't really sleep last night."

"Go to sleep, then," Brit said. She was really hoping Mikayla wouldn't.

"Maybe in a bit." Mikayla picked up a leaf and tossed it into the flames. It turned to pixels, floating upwards with the embers.

"Did you notice how it's fall now? All the leaves have changed and some of them are falling. I didn't know Suzanne had made seasons."

Brit laughed. "I don't think Suze knows either. This hasn't turned out quite like she imagined."

Mikayla tossed another leaf into the flames.

"That's putting it lightly." She hugged her knees to her chest.

"She's okay," Brit said. "I know she's okay. I mean, I don't know, but I know, you know?"

She winced at how stupid she sounded. But to her surprise Mikayla didn't make fun of her.

"I think I do know," Mikayla said. "If something had happened, we'd know, right? She couldn't have . . ."

"Died." The word stuck in Brit's throat.

"Yeah. She couldn't have. We aren't going to be too late."

"Shit, she probably escaped and she's leading an army to save us, I bet. Suze is the toughest chick in the world."

"In Io?"

"This world, our world, whatever. Remember Gretchen?"

Mikayla wrinkled her nose in disgust. "I swear I had forgotten her until you reminded me. Thanks for that."

Brit gave a mock bow. "You're welcome. But seriously, Gretchen was always such a bitch to Suzanne and Suzanne never cracked."

Mikayla thought about that for a second. "Well, she had us looking out for her."

"Maybe. But she handled shit freshman year without us having her back. And Ramses has nothing on Gretchen."

They laughed, and Brit felt it again. Their proximity. She could lean over and kiss her. Mikayla was only a foot, ten inches away.

"Where do you go at night?" Mikayla asked. "Where were you when Gemini attacked you?"

Brit froze. This, she hadn't seen coming.

"It's okay if you don't want to tell me. I guess I get it if you don't. But I woke up and you were gone."

"I was in Leo's garden when Gemini attacked me," Brit said.

"But it's been happening forever. Like when we were traveling across Altair, you'd be gone half the time at night."

She looked at Brit, the embers from the fire dancing reflected in her eyes.

"I have dreams," Brit said. "Suze said we wouldn't, but I keep having them. And they aren't all good ones. A bunch have been nightmares and weird shit about home. Fucked-up shit. And every time I woke up from one I would just go walk it off, get some air, clear my head."

Mikayla didn't say anything at first. Brit was afraid she had scared her.

"Don't worry," Mikayla said. "When we get Suzanne back, she'll be able to explain it, I'm sure."

Mikayla put a hand on Brit's knee. "But why didn't you tell me?" she asked. "You're my best friend."

"I didn't want you to worry," Brit said. "And, well, some of them were about you."

Brit looked away. She felt like the Lord of Lily Pads had just spit a whole bellyful of slime on her. Then Brit heard Mikayla giggle. "What were the dreams about me like?" she asked.

Oh, fuck it, Brit thought. "How about I show you?"

She leaned over and kissed Mikayla. Whatever happened tomorrow, it was going to be a good night.

Chapter 13

Two solid days of traveling. Suzanne was almost ready to collapse on her feet. They checked every village they saw, but the villages appeared to be empty. The latest village they came to was named Evandros, and it was empty as well. Not like the war-torn villages Suzanne had seen on the coasts of Altair and Pyxis, but absolutely empty, devoid of any sign of NPCs.

In fact, it looked like everyone in the village had decided to get up and leave at the same moment. Suzanne found half-eaten food in one house. In the town forge, items were abandoned mid-smithing. That made Suzanne uncomfortable, but it was better than the rows of statues she had seen in Altair. She wondered if the graying had spread to Ostia by now, and she wondered if that family had left.

They spent the night in Evandros. Suzanne was glad for the sleep mechanics as she didn't think she would have been able to get to sleep otherwise. The empty town felt haunted by its vanished inhabitants.

The next morning they set off as soon as they could, looking to put distance between the town and themselves. The season had changed in Pyxis as well as Altair. But the Pyxian savannah didn't have trees to lose their leaves. Instead, the tall grasses dried out, becoming tan and brittle. When Suzanne waded through a patch, the grass made a sound like snakes hissing. When Crux waded through, the grass pixelated, just like the Altairi leaves.

They made so much noise that Suzanne didn't see the weremonkeys until she stumbled into the pack.

The monsters attacked at once, hooting angrily. Weremonkeys looked like the missing link between humans and monkeys, miniature Bigfoots covered from their heads to the tips of their tails in matted brown fur. They fought with crude stone weapons, really just large rocks, but were fast enough to compensate for their technological shortcomings.

Still, they weren't much of a challenge. Crux never unstrapped his hammer, preferring to handle the agile weremonkeys with his gauntlets. Realizing they weren't doing much damage to the Dragoon, the monsters focused their efforts on Suzanne. Yet, she was just as fast as they were, and her weapons were much better.

She watched her XP trickle upwards with each new kill, only keeping half her mind on the battle at hand. She couldn't remember the last time she had fought a gang of monsters like this. A weremonkey tried to bite her on the arm. She elbowed it in the face, feeling nostalgic for the times when she'd grind XP with Brit and Mikayla.

Greatly reduced in number, the remaining wer-emonkeys took the better part of valor and split. They vanished into the savannah, hooting half-intelligible curses.

"Shall we keep going?" Crux asked.

Suzanne didn't say anything but trudged on through the grasses. Even if the NPCs were gone from Pyxis, at least there were still monsters.

Late in the afternoon, with the sky as golden as the plains, they finally found Glensia. Like all the Pyxian villages, the buildings in Glensia were yurts. They looked like round tents on wooden platforms, with open roofs to let out smoke. But unlike the other Pyxian villages, Glensia had not been abandoned.

No, the gray had seen to that. At a distance, Suzanne had thought the village was full of NPCs, but as they drew closer she saw that none of them were moving. She felt a knot in her stomach as they entered the town. She reached for a dagger to calm herself, and she noticed Crux had taken out his hammer.

"How did it spread so far?" Crux asked, examining the statue of a merchant. "I thought we were ahead of it."

Suzanne was wondering the same thing. Glensia was way far west of the Fens, so whatever was happening shouldn't have reached here yet. But then it occurred to Suzanne that the village was pretty far south in Pyxis. Maybe the gray wasn't spreading out from Fenhold, but north from the southern tip of Io. If that was the case, then it would make sense for Ostia to still be unaffected. Even if it was in Altair, Ostia was north of Glensia.

"Crux," she said, "I think I know what's happening."

"I know something too," he said. He pointed behind her with his massive, mailed fist.

Suzanne looked where he was pointing and saw a tuft of smoke leap up out of the roof of a yurt. The building was larger than the others, but not the largest building in Glensia. That had to be the village's Oratorium, which was on the opposite side of the town square.

Suzanne held a finger up to her lips. Crux understood and tiptoed after Suzanne.

The windows of the yurt had been blocked out. But clearly someone was inside. Suzanne heard the bang of hammers. Was an NPC forging in this village? How had they avoided turning gray?

She stood on one side of the door, and Crux on the other.

"On three," Suzanne whispered. "One, two . . . "

The door of the yurt burst open. Before Suzanne could react, she was staring down the flat, broad blade of a scimitar.

"I do not know who you are," Burgrave said. Then he stopped, realizing that he did in fact know who it was.

"Suzanne?" he asked. "Can it be you? And Crux? How did you find me?"

Burgrave spoke without any of the usual officiousness in his voice. In its place was weariness. The long chain earrings he normally wore were gone, as was the sash adorned with the Altairi insignia. His normal cloak, gray as smoke, had been replaced with plain traveling garb. He looked very much like he was trying not to attract attention to himself. Suzanne thought he looked years older than when she had seen him last.

"Burgrave, I—" Crux began, but Burgrave waved him off.

"There will be time later," Burgrave said. He stared at Suzanne with his unfathomable misty eyes. "How did you find me? And why?"

"Crux mentioned you were from here. He came to find you. I came for the key."

As always, Burgrave's face remained impassive. "Very well," he said. "Follow me."

He took off without waiting to see if Suzanne

and Crux were following. Suzanne jogged after him. She had to keep up with Burgrave, she had to keep up with the key.

The diminutive NPC came to a halt beside the Oratorium. It was nowhere near as grand as the one in Vale, but it was still the largest building in Glensia.

"Wait out here," he said to Crux. Crux saluted and didn't question the order.

Burgrave pulled the door open and slipped inside.

"Hey!" Suzanne said. "Wait up!"

It was completely dark in the Oratorium. Suzanne walked forward, her hands out in front of her, until she heard Burgrave, his voice like gravel, utter one word.

"Stop."

She froze. Even with her limited vision she could make out the point of Burgrave's sword hovering in front of her face.

"Do you know what this key is?" Burgrave's

voice was calm, as steady as his sword hand. That did little to relieve Suzanne's anxiety.

"Yes," she said.

"And how did you get free? The last I heard you were still Ramses's prisoner."

"Crux freed me. He decided he wouldn't serve Ramses anymore."

"Why?"

"You know why," Suzanne replied.

Burgrave lowered his sword. "I do," he said.

"My turn. What are you doing here?"

"I thought . . . " Burgrave began. He sighed and pulled a torch from his inventory. Igniting it, the room was cast in a flickering light. Suzanne could make out the features of the statues. These weren't like the transfixed Citizens outside. These were made by Pyxians to commemorate their dead, a permanent marker for pixelated loved ones.

"I thought I might see my parents. But of course they are not here. They died in Altair, and so will not be remembered. I hoped I might find someone here who remembered them, but none do."

Suddenly Suzanne realized what Burgrave had been doing in the forge. He was trying to make statues to commemorate his parents.

"I do not know what has happened to these Citizens," he said. "It is a mockery of the Oratorium, a mockery of death."

"It's Xenos," Suzanne.

"Xenos?" Burgrave pronounced the name with hatred. "Ramses does not know what he has unleashed upon Io."

"Ramses is dead," Suzanne said.

Burgrave took a step back in surprise. "How?"

She didn't say anything, but he seemed to understand. Burgrave had abandoned Ramses, but after serving the king for so long Suzanne didn't know how he would take the news.

"I hope he has found peace," was all the NPC said.

The torchlight flickered "Show me the key," Suzanne said.

A bit of gold flashed in the darkness. Suzanne saw a vein of Energite traveling down the length of the key, green against the gold. Just as quickly, Burgrave stowed the item back in his robe.

"Why'd you leave Fenhold?"

"I assume that is obvious," Burgrave replied.

"Okay, fine. But why'd you take the key?"

"I thought it would prevent Xenos from using his powers. It appears I was mistaken."

The tunnel sloped upwards. Suzanne saw another bramble grille covering the exit.

"Who is Xenos? Where did he come from?"

"I do not know. One day after you fled your trial, when King Ramses exited the Oracle Chamber, the hooded one was with him. Since then, he has not strayed far from the King's side."

Burgrave hesitated. "At first I thought he was like you."

"Like me?"

"Like you and Mikayla and Brit. He was not from Altair or Pyxis, that much I could tell immediately. He . . . he knew things about our countries, knew more than anyone should know. All of Io is known to him. It reminded me of my first encounters with you. How you seemed to know more than your years should allow."

Suzanne shuddered at the comparison. Not for the first time she wondered if someone else had found their way into Io, and if that person was playing as Xenos. The hooded NPC was marked by an NPC icon, but someone skilled enough at coding could have easily faked that.

"After the defeat at The Floating Eye, Ramses was furious. He wanted to destroy you and Pyxis more than anything. And this Xenos offered him the power to do so. They made some compact, its specifics I know not. But since that day the hooded one's influence has grown while the King's diminished. I left, hoping to find your companions and undo what he had done."

"I can fix things," Suzanne said. "But I need that key. I need to be able to get into the Oracle Chamber."

Burgrave stared at her. "Very well," he said. "I am without a king to serve. It appears once more I must decide which course is the correct one."

The key appeared again in his hand. He pressed it into Suzanne's palm. It felt cool, but pulsed, like a current was passing from the key into her body. She didn't know what to say, but Burgrave didn't wait for her. He thrust the torch into her other hand and walked out of the Oratorium into the sunset.

Chapter 14

Mikayla woke up first, still a little giddy from the previous night. Physical sensations in Io were always a little off, but with Brit everything felt right. For once, it was nice being with someone who liked her for herself. Not the personality she projected, but who she was beneath all that. And who knew her better than Brit?

Brit slumbered on the bedroll, the corners of her mouth twitching. Mikayla watched her for a minute, wondering if she was dreaming, what she could be dreaming of. Then she stole from the tent out into the dawn.

The season had changed—she was almost cold. She equipped her armor just to warm herself, but its presence was still reassuring. She wondered what it would be like when she didn't spend every day with her swords strapped to her side.

Mallon was poking at the fire, letting it go out.

"Morning," Mikayla said.

Mallon smiled and stretched. "Morning to you too. Anything go bump in the night?" She gave Mikayla a roguish wink.

Mikayla felt her face growing hot. "When are we heading out?" she asked, trying to change the subject.

"In a minute. Thought I would let the princess and the others sleep a little longer. Can't say the next time they'll have the luxury."

"Mallon," Mikayla said, lowering her voice. "You don't really think Suzanne is working with Xenos, do you? I mean you know her. You know she wouldn't do that."

The NPC frowned, toying with her long braid.

"I suppose I do know her, least as well as I know you. What I mean is that I know what I know, what I see, and hear. Everything else I can only guess on."

"But," she said, barreling on through the crest-fallen look spreading on Mikayla's face. "If I was to guess, I would say Suzanne is Suzanne."

Alphonse emerged from his tent fully dressed and equipped for travel. He gave them a curt nod and walked over to Lynx's tent. In another few minutes, they were all ready.

"Be safe," Rigel said. "You lot won't have me looking out for you." He hugged Lynx, bowed low to the others, and set off north toward the mountains and Vale.

"He will manage," Alphonse said. "We should go."

They went. The party swept across the rocky Pyxian plains, cresting the hills and crossing the valleys as they headed toward Glensia. Mikayla found herself walking close to Brit, finding excuses to stumble and have Brit catch her hand. It was the

most obvious thing in the world, both worlds—
how had she missed it for so long?

But there were other matters, more pressing. Matters with claws and teeth. The kobolds Mikayla had last seen watching them with leery eyes were out in force. For half a day, they were content to keep their distance, surveying the party with cold-blooded interest. They kept their short swords sheathed but never let too much space grow between them and the girls.

The party rested beneath the shade of spindly palm trees near a small pond.

"Should we deal with them?" Mallon asked. She had just returned from scouting and reported that the kobolds numbered in the dozens.

"I think we can leave them alone," Brit replied. "The ones on our way to New Pyxia didn't bother us."

Lynx was studying a map of Pyxis. "The village isn't too far south of here," she said. "We should make it there well before sunset."

"You think it's safe?" Brit asked. "What if Leo's put a bounty on us."

Lynx looked unsure. "I do not think Pyxians would betray us. They are not like Altairi. They will not attack us simply because Leo commands."

"We cannot risk your safety on strangers," Alphonse said.

"These aren't strangers," Mallon said. "They're Pyxians, same as you and me."

"Why don't me and Mikayla go check it out?" Brit suggested. "You three can hang out here. We'll come back and get you if everything's cool."

"What if you do not return?" Alphonse asked.

Brit shrugged. "Maybe don't stick around for what got us."

And if we find Suzanne, Mikayla thought, *we might not come back at all.*

There were no objections to the idea so Mikayla and Brit immediately set out. Off in the distance, Mikayla saw the kobolds following them. But as they neared Glensia, the kobolds fell back, eventually disappearing into the dry savannah grass.

When she reported that to Brit, Brit laughed. "Guess they went looking for easier prey."

Mikayla wished she felt so sure herself. The kobolds made her uneasy. Now that they were gone she figured she would feel better, but the knot in her stomach remained.

Seeing how worried she looked, Brit reached out and squeezed her hand. "You okay?"

"Yeah," Mikayla said. But she wasn't even convincing herself.

When they were a hundred yards off from the village of Glensia, Mikayla realized it was quiet. Too quiet to be full of NPCs. A single trail of smoke was visible, spiraling up from the center of the village, but there were no other signs of life.

It was only when they entered the town that Mikayla saw the statues.

They looked like statues from an Oratorium, but what were they doing outside? And besides, the Oratorium statues were memorials for NPCs. Why had all these statues been carved to look frightened?

Mikayla wasn't the only one uncomfortable.

"What's going on?" Brit whispered. Her question hung in the air. They remained close together as they walked through the village.

"Looks like Glensia's a bust," Brit said. "Let's get out of here. This place gives me the creeps."

Then Mikayla saw him. It was Crux, the massive Dragoon from The Floating Eye. He was sitting on the steps of the Oratorium, idly tossing his enormous war hammer from hand to hand. What was he doing in Pyxis?

Crux had seen them too. And he waved his hammer over his head.

"Watch out for that thing," Brit said. "I'm pretty sure I still have bruises from our fight on The Floating Eye."

Mikayla nodded. Crux was one of Ramses's stronger minions. And if he was around that meant there were definitely going to be more Altairi troops.

Brit took out her halberd and began to charge at Crux. She was halfway to the Dragoon when Mikayla saw another NPC slip out of the Oratorium.

She couldn't believe what she was seeing. That had to be Burgrave!

From the way he stopped and stared back, Mikayla was pretty sure Burgrave was just as surprised to see her. If both Burgrave and Crux were around, that meant that Ramses had to be up to something.

Mikayla drew her swords. Well, she had beaten Burgrave once before. She'd just have to do it again.

Burgrave's scimitar appeared in his hand.

Mikayla saw Brit slam into Crux. Her attack knocked the bigger Dragoon off his feet. But last time they fought, it had taken Brit half an hour to wear Crux down. That wasn't time they had right now.

"Burgrave," Mikayla said. "Prepare yourself."

Much to her surprise, the NPC did the exact opposite. He lay his scimitar flat on the ground and held his hands up in the air.

"You will find we are not enemies," he said. He nodded toward the Oratorium.

"Crux!" he shouted. Mikayla looked over and saw Crux freeze, mid-swing. "Put your weapon down. These are Suzanne's friends, remember?"

"What's Suze got to do with this?" Brit asked.

In reply, Burgrave simply pointed once more to the Oratorium.

At first Mikayla thought it might be Gemini. In the shadowy Oratorium, it was hard to be sure. It didn't help that when they came in, the character drew a pair of daggers like she was ready to use them.

But then Mikayla saw the green icon over

Suzanne's head, and Suzanne said, "No fucking way," and then Mikayla knew it was her.

"You're crushing me!" Suzanne gasped, struggling for air through one of Brit's bear-hugs. Brit let her go.

"You shithead!" Brit laughed. "We were crazy worried! We went all the way across Io trying to get help for you, and you just freed yourself? You could have saved us the trouble!"

Suzanne rubbed her sides gingerly. "Sorry to disappoint you."

"We were worried," Mikayla said quietly. She hugged Suzanne, though not quite as tightly.

"I was worried about you guys too," Suzanne said. Mikayla listened with wonder as Suzanne explained how Crux had freed her and how they had met up with Burgrave.

"But listen," she said, "that's not important. Xenos, you know, the hooded NPC?"

"You mean the mind-control guy?" Brit asked.

Suzanne gasped. "How'd you know?"

Mikayla shared what had happened to Leo. Even if he was just an NPC, she thought Suzanne took the news of her ex getting mind-controlled remarkably well.

"That's what he did to Ramses," Suzanne said, when she finished. "I watched him to do it the night I got captured."

"You mean Ramses isn't really a dick?" Brit asked.

Mikayla watched Suzanne's face grow somber.

"He's dead," she said. "I killed him."

"No fucking way," Brit said.

They stood in silence for a moment, remembering the NPC and all he had done to them. Then they were done remembering so they left the Oratorium.

"What are these statues, anyway?" Brit asked. "They're super sketchy."

"Citizens," Suzanne said. "Xenos, he—he did something to them. I don't know what. But it's spreading."

"Just when I thought he couldn't get any screwier," Mikayla said.

They walked around Glensia. Burgrave and Crux gave them space, but even then they didn't say much. They didn't have to. For the three of them, simply being together again was enough.

Eventually, Suzanne stopped.

"Okay, I know I was in a dungeon for a while," she said, "but what's up with the two of you?"

Mikayla realized that she and Brit were holding hands.

"Nothing," Brit said, grinning wide.

"Seriously," Suzanne said. "What's going on?"

"We, uh," Brit began. She looked at Mikayla, helpless.

"We're together," Mikayla said.

"Yeah, duh," Suzanne replied. Mikayla saw her eyes light up as she understood.

"Wait, what? Really?"

Mikayla nodded.

"But . . . " Mikayla had rarely seen Suzanne

so confused. She braced herself for the worst, but Suzanne shook her head and smiled.

"Well, whatever. I guess this means I have to be the one to point out all the problems with Brit."

"Ha ha," Brit said.

"No, I'm serious. We did this for every idiot she had a crush on back in the real world. Mikayla, this Brit chick is terrible for you. A Swiftblade and a Dragoon? Hardly what I'd call a balanced party."

Mikayla rolled her eyes. "Tough shit," she said. "I really like this one."

They all laughed. Brit gave Mikayla's hand a little squeeze.

"By the way," Mikayla said, "Lynx, Alphonse, and Mallon are waiting for us. We were supposed to go get them once we checked the village out. They're heading to the Pyxian camp to raise an army against Leo. I'm sure they'll be stoked to have you with us."

She thought it was best not to mention that Alphonse thought Suzanne had turned.

"Let's just head back to Zenith City," Suzanne said. "They won't need their revolution if we can just fix the game. We need to get back to the Oracle Chamber."

Mikayla groaned. "Not this again. Look, you couldn't get it open, okay? No one is blaming you."

"Well, I'm blaming you," Brit said.

"Very funny," Suzanne said. "No shut up and listen. Burgrave stole the key to the Oracle Chamber. And, well, I got it from him. So it looks like I can get it open after all."

Mikayla had never seen Suzanne look so pleased with herself. Well, no, that wasn't quite true. But the only other time Suzanne had seemed so smug was right after they put on the TII and entered Io for the first time.

"What are you saying?" Mikayla asked.

"I'm saying we can get into the Oracle Chamber," Suzanne said. "There's a way out of here," she said, reaching into her inventory. In the flat of her palm was a golden key. "I'm saying I found the way home."

Nearby was one of the Citizens. The three of them were so caught up with each other's company, so happy to know there was a way out of Io, that they missed it when the statue began to change. Its skin grew rougher, the nails sharpening into claws. The look of horror stamped on the young man's face deepened into a snarl. Fangs grew from incisors, and the eyes turned bloodshot and wild.

And then the statue moved.

Chapter 15

Seconds earlier, the Citizen had been as still as a statue. Suzanne was telling Brit and Mikayla about the key to the Oracle Chamber when she heard something move behind her. It sounded like stone scraping against stone, like nothing else she had heard in Io. When she turned around, the NPC jumped at her.

Yet, was it an NPC? The creature was deformed, not just by its expression but by some other force. Its body was rough and gray like it was made of concrete. Suzanne barely registered that the Citizen lacked a twirling gray icon which marked it as an NPC. She was too busy defending herself against those claws.

She slashed at its face with her dagger, but the blade bounced off without leaving a scratch. It raked at her with its claws; she ducked and slashed at its stomach. Sparks flew from the contact but no damage was done. When the creature lunged for her again Suzanne jumped to the side and tried to perform a Backstab. The blade of her dagger snapped off as she drove it into the creature's flinty hide.

The creature turned and snatched at her, but Mikayla stabbed at its wrist with one of her swords. Again, the blade failed to make a dent, but it pushed the claws away from Suzanne.

"Move!" Suzanne heard Brit shout, and she jumped back. Brit swung her halberd overhead, slamming the axe-blade onto the creature's shoulder. The force of her blow knocked the Citizen to its knees, but it also shattered the head of the halberd. Still, even if the gargoyle couldn't be cut, it could be bludgeoned. Brit smashed the pole of her halberd into the creature again and again until it was merely pixels.

"What the fuck was that?" Brit asked, as the shaft pixelated in her hands. She grabbed another weapon out of her inventory. "What the hell just happened here?"

Suzanne had no idea. She walked toward the other frozen Citizens. None of the others had transformed. They still looked like statues, not like the gray monstrosity that had just attacked her.

"Suzanne! Get away from them!" Mikayla shouted. Suzanne glanced over at Mikayla, who was standing with Brit a safe distance away from the Citizens. She saw Burgrave and Crux come around a corner.

"We heard sounds of battle," Burgrave said. "Where is the enemy?"

Suzanne gestured toward the remaining Citizens and walked over to meet them. "I didn't see it happen. One second they were just standing there and the next second one attacked me."

All five of them, player and NPC, watched the statues with suspicious eyes. None of the others moved.

"They are just statues," Crux said, puzzled.

Suzanne sighed. "I know, but one of them changed. We need to get rid of these things before any of the others turn."

Brit nodded and took a few steps toward the Citizens.

"Stop," Burgrave said. Suzanne could hear steel in his voice and it frightened her. "They are not things. Those are the Citizens of Glensia. I thought when they were statues that was monstrous enough. But to destroy the helpless afflicted . . . there are no words for such a heinous act."

"I can think of a few."

Everyone turned to see a second Suzanne standing in the center of the village.

"Gemini," Brit hissed.

Gemini? Suzanne didn't understand. The NPC standing in the town square looked almost exactly like her. It was like looking into a mirror, except Suzanne was an Infiltrator, not an Assassin. She'd played as an Assassin while testing the game out, but hadn't touched that character since. But she knew Gemini's voice, and the NPC was Gemini, no matter what she looked like.

"Yes," Gemini gloated. "Me. Here I was, ready to finish off Brit and Mikayla, when who should show up but two more traitors?"

Suzanne saw Burgrave draw his sword. Crux hefted his hammer.

"And Suzanne, of course. Tired of Ramses's hospitality? I hear you took care of that little annoyance for us."

The Assassin strolled toward them, tossing one of her knives in the air. It spun a lazy three-hundred-and-sixty degrees before she caught it by the handle.

"You should run while you can," Brit said. "You don't have a bunch of guards to save your ass this time."

Gemini laughed. "That's cute. Hey Burgrave, remember when you said you didn't have words for this? Well, I can think of a few. How about 'a taste of things to come'?"

Suzanne heard the scraping sound again and whirled around to see the Citizens transforming. Fingers stretched into talons. The flesh tightened across new grown muscles as mouths widened into fierce howls which displayed razor-sharp fangs. Whatever compassion had been trapped in the Citizen statues drained away, replaced by a vicious aspect.

There had been twenty Citizens in the town square. Now there were twenty gray creatures, flexing their new claws as they formed ranks and marched toward Gemini. Suzanne had no idea how the Assassin was controlling the creatures, but that didn't really matter right now. Brit, Mikayla, and Suzanne were barely able to handle one of the creatures. And now there were twenty, along with Gemini.

"Are you going to charge in?" the Assassin asked. "Or are we going to have to come get you?"

She tossed her knife one more time, catching it by the blade. She whipped it at Suzanne, who stepped to the side. The knife sliced through the yurt behind her like it was warm butter.

"Well, shit," Brit said. "No time like the present."

She led the charge, Suzanne yelling with the others as they followed her. The creatures surged forward, rending claws at the ready.

"Now, Crux!" Burgrave yelled. The Dragoon's hammer rose high, glowing white hot. "Crater!" boomed the giant, and he brought the hammerhead down. The impact sent a shockwave out in all directions, knocking the nearest creatures off their feet.

Yet even more were pouring into the village. Suzanne realized why all the other towns in Pyxis had been empty. Gemini must have been to Evandros and the others, recruiting these creatures for her army.

Six of the gargoyles came running out from

behind the forge. Brit turned to face them and Suzanne stayed with her, unsure of what she could do. All her melee attacks depended on slicing and stabbing and they were all useless against the Citizens. Brit tackled the nearest gargoyle and rammed her fist into its face until it stayed down. Another charged at Suzanne, and she dove to the side. But when she got back up to her feet, she saw that the creatures had cordoned her off from Brit and the rest of the party.

Which left her alone with Gemini.

"You know," Gemini said, "I'm really happy you escaped. If I had to kill you while you were in chains that wouldn't have been a challenge."

She slashed at Suzanne. Suzanne caught Gemini's blade on her own and turned the attack away. She dropped her dagger and grabbed for a throwing knife from her belt, but the Assassin kicked it out of her hand.

"Not that this is gonna be a challenge either," Gemini taunted.

Keep talking, Suzanne thought. Suzanne had never beaten the Assassin, but she was done playing by Io rules. Gemini might know every trick in Io's playbook, but Suzanne had a whole other world to draw from.

The Assassin leapt close, stabbing at Suzanne's stomach. Suzanne jumped to the side and grabbed for Gemini's hair. She found a handful and pulled.

In the real world, the clump might have come loose. But in Io that wouldn't happen. Suzanne yanked Gemini down to the ground and then dropped her knee onto the Assassin's chest. She didn't let up, stabbing the Assassin half a dozen times before Gemini was able to force her off with a kick.

Suzanne bounced back up. "You aren't shit," she said. She hurled two knives at the Assassin who dove behind one of the yurts for protection.

Then two of the creatures broke off from the cordon and attacked Suzanne. With nowhere else to go, she climbed up to the roof of the forge, out of range of the Citizens' claws. She searched the battle for Gemini, but the Assassin was nowhere to be seen.

Suzanne glanced up at her health. Less than a quarter remained. Scouring the buildings for Gemini, she rifled through her inventory for a healing item. Her hand closed around some herbs and she shoved them against her chest, bringing her back up to half of her health. Not a lot, but it would have to do.

Suzanne heard a shout of pain and saw Brit disappear beneath a dog pile of the creatures. She hopped from one roof to another until she was right above the mass of gray bodies.

"Brit, watch out!" she yelled as she readied a Naphtha Bomb. She jumped off the roof and threw the bomb down at the creatures.

The bomb exploded, spraying pixels everywhere. Brit finished off the Citizens that weren't immediately killed.

"Where's Gemini?" Brit growled as she withdrew a third halberd from her inventory.

"I don't know," Suzanne said. "But we've got to help the others."

Brit looked around and nodded. They ran to where Mikayla and Burgrave were fighting back to back, doing their best to parry the creatures' slashes. With Brit and Suzanne joining in the fight, the tide turned. Crux reemerged by the inn, smashing the gargoyles to pieces as he cleared a path to the rest of the party. Slowly, the party began to make progress, whittling the Citizens down until they were no longer trapped in a defensive position.

We can do this! Suzanne thought as she lobbed a Naphtha Bomb at a pair of Citizens. There were only a dozen of the creatures now. Crux led the way past the forge, knocking off another of the gargoyles. The creatures could sense the tide of battle turning and had begun to disengage, reforming in the town square.

"Crux take the front," Suzanne said. "Brit, you're next to him. We're going to rush them and finish this!"

And then she felt the blade.

It was different from before. As Gemini stabbed her from inside the forge, slicing through the thin canvas wall, Suzanne felt no pain.

She had never really felt pain in Io. Whenever she saw herself about to get hit by a weapon, whenever she registered a health bar drop, her brain created the physical sensation of getting stabbed or cut or bludgeoned. In a way, Suzanne did it to herself.

But when Gemini used Backstab, Suzanne didn't feel anything physically. She felt surprise and fear, because her health bar went from yellow to red—to empty all at once.

She looked down at her hand and saw it rippling. She was dimly aware of Brit roaring something, some kind of commotion behind her as Gemini cut her way free and fled off into the falling dusk.

Suzanne fell to her knees. Her whole body shivered. Not a shiver from the cold, but the shiver of every bit of her undulating and breaking apart.

She saw Mikayla crouching over her, shoving

healing items at her, but of course they'd have no effect. You had to have health to be healed. Maybe that was a dumb design. There was always room for improvement.

Her hand was the first to go. She watched her fingers widen into clouds of pixels and then disperse.

"There must be some kind of glitch," Suzanne said. "I feel totally fine."

And then she was pixels.

And then she was gone.